Today Ended an Hour Ago

The Art of Impersonating Yourself

Tessia-Yasmine

outskirts press

Today Ended An Hour Ago
The Art of Impersonating Yourself
All Rights Reserved.
Copyright © 2023 Tessia-Yasmine
v2.0

This is a work of fiction. Names, characters, businesses, places, events, locales, and incidents are either the products of the author's imagination or used in a fictitious manner. Any resemblance to actual persons, living or dead, or actual events is purely coincidental.

The opinions expressed in this manuscript are solely the opinions of the author and do not represent the opinions or thoughts of the publisher. The author has represented and warranted full ownership and/or legal right to publish all the materials in this book.

This book may not be reproduced, transmitted, or stored in whole or in part by any means, including graphic, electronic, or mechanical without the express written consent of the publisher except in the case of brief quotations embodied in critical articles and reviews.

Outskirts Press, Inc.
http://www.outskirtspress.com

ISBN: 978-1-9772-6218-9

Cover Photo © 2023 Dreamstime. All rights reserved - used with permission.

Outskirts Press and the "OP" logo are trademarks belonging to Outskirts Press, Inc.

PRINTED IN THE UNITED STATES OF AMERICA

"There are more Starbucks than libraries, and people have more clothes than books."

In dedication to my sculptors

Based on true events

Any events placed cannot be used as evidence in a court of law

Preface

SINE METU

The elderly, pungent and poised, radiant or frail, are signifiers. Symbolic representations of the time unknowingly remind us that if I can make it this far, so can you. When you walk down a street looking for something to fill the time, be it beer, company, or a nice red wine, look for the elderly sitting, standing, or demanding the best, for their time is a prize until they reach their demise.

Dennis A. Bjorkland, Jie Dong, James T. Hammes, Jorge Iglesias, and David Richard Kaup were major white-collar criminals who lived life with a little extra spice. They didn't fear the law because they were above it. Vocabulary consists of semantics and technicalities falling into the grey areas of economically driven ideals. The difference between right and wrong does not come from the law of man or God; it is bestowed upon us through something valued as much greater. Money.

Most parents want to shelter their children from the cruel world surrounding them, keeping them close to home so they may never stray too far from the beaten path. The home was something inconsistent, the beaten path not nearly as clear as thought to be; you could call this a coming-of-age novel, but the idea of one miraculous event making you an adult was hardly plausible, far more relatable to say a series of unfortunate events or a slap in the face saying this is reality and sometimes shit happens. I invite you into the daily crusades of my life—the unfortunate events, the slaps to the face, the animate pains, but also the prosperous lessons learned.

I ran away so much that my mom put deadbolts in our big oak doors; she never let me forget that. The first time she found me was in the middle of the playground, staring up at the sky, probably deciding whether or not I liked clouds. To this day, I am still unsure. The farthest was to the aquarium, sneaking past security to the shark tanks and sitting and observing until someone came up and asked me where my parents were. They were at home. He asked who accompanied me, and I said nobody. It seemed where they were was unimportant; it mattered more where they were not.

At the age of four, my mom was arrested again. Which time was this? No one could really say. We all lost count. She was like the men listed above—wanted for their untrappable minds. There isn't much to say about it, like why she was there or for how long; just whatever needed to be hidden when the rooms were raided could be tucked away in my pull-ups. Maybe that's what the Huggies commercial means when they say I'm a big kid now.

The aftermath, a long dirt path to the facility, and her sitting behind that glass window in black and white striped pyjamas. Little, meticulously paved cutouts were drawn to break the divide so we could speak to one another. Fixated on those absences of space, anticipating a world of danger seeping through those tiny little holes. She was home a few days later, and the thought became a distant memory. Growing up in a family such as mine, you find yourself asking a lot: Where do my loyalties lie? Does loyalty hide amongst the expectations of who can offer more, or are we burdened by something deeper?

Our surroundings form expectations, but what if your surroundings keep changing? How does one decide whether or not to feed or starve the idea of expectancy, and doesn't it seem like the problems we procure always revolve around the same matter regardless of the setting? At what point do you look in the mirror and say, *Behold the problem*. Is that when we come of age? After handling the same problem repeatedly and finally accepting that we lack control over the dimensions of our insanity. The conscious self can be taught to use the chaos we crave. In this story, you'll come to realise that no matter how ever evolving our mentality may be, the child inside of us will always be whispering sweet words in the corner of the room to the man in the mirror, sometimes with tears in their eyes, begging us to listen.

Where are you from? What a nuisance of a question. Do you mean where I was born or what genetics create my ethnically ambiguous features and toned complexion, or perhaps it is my cultural practises you wish to know about? I am from the outside, an outsider with no claim or place. Only the cliche gratification of claiming home is where the heart is when, in reality, you don't know where your heart is at all, just that it's always with you, even though little pieces are left scattered around the world. In turn, wherever my head falls, that is home for the physical self. The heart and head are encompassed in the same shell.

When you are young and chaos is normal for you, you expect other people to find it normal as well. But, as I've learned, there are levels of chaos. The complexity of it falls along the lines of what can and cannot be controlled by thine own actions.

Judgement is one of our basic instincts. Political Judgement is like rust; it spreads, capturing those bound by fear of societal deterioration. In the world of elitist criminals, many have a deep-rooted god complex, for they are ones that beseech judgement. Erasing moral lines to best suit their *hobbies* and eating away at the shiny metal cuffs you try to hold onto it with. It is not what you do; it is what they can prove, and that is the leg upon which their thrones rest.

Born in a small town with smaller-minded people, the suffocating desert borders never felt like home. It was a truly foreign feeling to try and recall any memories from those days, as if I lived with a stranger hosting my body. The Mesa, Arizona Hospital, on 29th April 1999, delivered a little girl named Teaha-Maria Ladas, that's me. From the outside, everything seemed pleasant; we were just the blackish family down the street who left the Christmas lights out far past December.

My mother was our family's core and did not need

a simple life; she did not come from one and thus felt no comfort in it. She was a masochist of the mind. We lived in a great house in a gated community on the lake, with not one but two docks, our pool accessorised by a seven-foot rock waterfall, a boat, and countless costly cars. We even had our tiny golf course on the side of the house with the fake grass, so it never looked dead. Like that fake grass, my family covered our secrets, like the decaying earth underneath, with a faux-green finish. Five out of the seven days, my father was away in the Greenlands of California. That is, of course, when it wasn't always on fire. It's amazing the way things look when you're a kid. You always want what is out of reach. Sitting in the window with my sister, we watched my father leave at all hours of the day and night every week for six years in his green Jeep Wrangler, then for another four years in the red Jeep Sahara that he so generously exchanged with the women next door. Pleading with him to take me too sometimes worked. His work place was my second house, the firehouse, where I had no standard one or two uncles but 20, who filled me with copious amounts of chocolate and laughter upon every visit and, yes, sliding down the fire pole. One of the secretaries had a typewriter, and while my father worked, they would assign me interview jobs around the building, concocting ridiculous stories solely for my entertainment. On training days, they would cast me as a lifeless victim in need of rescue. CPR certified since the age of six. This was the beginning of my poor attendance record.

My father, Marc, is a simple man with simple wants. At least, that is what he conveyed to the world. What happened beneath his surface was unknown. I'm not even sure he knew. A man who used to tower over me with stature and dark piercing eyes got promoted to fire chief in Burlingame, California, by leading the merger set forth by Hillsborough and Burlingame and expanding it to Millbrae and San Bruno, resulting in the Central County Fire Department, which in some parts of town had the clean, smooth asphalt with no cracks and the houses with the big candy bars during Halloween—way to go, Daddy. My mother's name, you could pick a few, changed as often as she did. Shaughn, since that was the name she signed my birth certificate with.

In 2010, my mother, sister, and I moved to California to witness his rise and rebuild the rusty bridge that the family had become. Now, what happens when a broken man meets a broken woman? They make broken babies. In this world, it is easier to buy something new than fix something old, and in a year, my family will soon prove this true again. Life was in overdrive, and that became my comfort.

When you know what it's like to be something, you know what it means not to be it anymore. Like being happy knowing that you are no longer, then forgetting what it was like to be happy at all, being in love, or comfortable. For me, it was violence. There comes a time when a feeling is found so frequently it disappears altogether.

Violence is the seamstress for progress in our world, a world that contests those who do not follow its norms yet relies on their ability to drive it forward.

Unfortunately, this isn't the story of a girl who found success in her anger. That every bloody knuckle to the wall was simply practise for her future career as a championship boxer. The girl in this story dies a hundred times over. Every mistake and downfall is like a hurricane wiping out everything down to the last brick, all in search of the eye.

Chapter One

Dreams leaked from open wounds will drown in the rivers in which they were born

18 December 2012

White linen sheets that smelled of cleaning detergent, tucked and crisp, unstained. Hotel beds are luxury hospitals to us—a place to escape when we need healing or hiding. There were times when we would be checked in for months; those are faded memories now.

My sister and I weren't the friendly types of siblings; she was more closely related to a hibernating bear. Laci, the older one, shackled to her continuity, grunting and moaning more than she held a conversation, but stupidly gifted. We shared a bed, which was about the only thing we shared. A subtle movement was quickly noticed, resulting in an elbow to my ribcage, shoving me off the bed. Space was always more of a demand than a request.

The hotel opens at its centre as a dome-shaped home for its temporary visitors, inviting intrusive thoughts of falling from great heights. Overindulged in plastic greenery, it was a sterilised tropical paradise. People were eating in the little engulfed cafe below. My parents' room is adjacent to ours; it is funny just how alone you can feel in a hotel, even with neighbours a mere few feet away.

Doors always seem bigger when you're on the outside of them. *"Hey, baby."* The most unacknowledged perk of being a tall woman, specifically a six-foot-tall mother, is that at 11 years old, this woman can still pick up all my 95 pounds and carry me to bed.

Her luggage was scattered across the room, making it seem like this had been our home for months instead of the two days we had spent lounging and watching movies. The land line rang in a monotone hum until the kitchen staff had time to place our order.

Breakfast of wet fruit that's just a little too colourful with buttermilk pancakes; they always smell better than they taste.

The room was bare by the time we finished packing,

double-checking phone chargers, and adding the extra shampoo bottles.

My parents' room is still as messy as the day we arrived. My mother's focus is drawn to her work. Work that sometimes caused problems, problems we didn't talk about. The room was cleaned up well enough in a hurry, but the bed wasn't made.

We should have made the bed.

Three suitcases and two backpacks for a two-day stay in a hotel 30 minutes from where we lived. Our reason for being here was unclear. It was almost Christmas, so events occurred without explanation. We walked by the plants observed from above to the big doors leading outside. This moment was over, and a new one was beginning on the other side.

My grandpa was sitting on his porch, dressed in his sheriff's uniform, with no intention of acknowledging our arrival other than a crack in his smile. Our house was behind his, next to the pool, under a giant magnolia tree. He planted a sapling for my grandmother, and 30 years later, it stood 20 feet tall, shedding. It smelled of rainy days, even when the sun caused droughts. It was

Sunday, and my face should have been buried in books getting ready for school tomorrow, but the television was too tempting. I was lost for hours in the nonsense.

Around seven, the phone rang, lagging and static; she was driving, only one part of the hill hides, weakening the cell service.

"On my way home, pack a backpack with your passport and some clothes. Tell Laci to do the same." Our rule in the house was to do what you were told, and then once you did it, you may ask why. Something was wrong, even though random trips were normal. The hairs on my neck stood up as my mother's instructions were relayed from down the hall. She huffed in protest of this unexpected vacation and took the phone from me, but my mother said something to Laci, and she left the room, leaving me behind, with only a gesture of a stern head nod which, in our family, means, "Do what you are told".

My sisters rapidly pacing footsteps in the background and me chasing after them because we had rules didn't mean we would always follow them. *"Lala, what did she say?"*

"Just do what she said; we gotta go." A direct response. *"Okay."*

Her hand lingered in the grip of the phone. My pink backpack, alongside hers, was dragged outside. It had been years since my mother's last arrest; there was a feeling of familiarity at this moment. Not panic, just impatience. If something were to happen, let it be known now.

Our Jeep Liberty pulled into the driveway, still running. *"Put our bags in the car and wait."* Rigid commands to deaf soldiers standing in a rustic pathway.

My mom's head bobbed up and down as she filled the boot with laptops and binders, our eyes meeting only for a second. *"Now is not the time, Teaha."* An uncomforting voice. The silence was uneasy and flooded the car as she began to drive away, with our house disappearing behind us.

An hour passed of mindlessly staring out the window. Sliding my fingers across the dusty dashboard, I said, *"Mom..."* More silence. My hand rested on her shoulder from the passenger's seat, an indisputable presence. *"We're heading to the border. I left my wallet at the hotel, and your father went to get it. He was approached by undercover police and probably taken in for questioning."*

Shit. "Shit." She smiled just a little. It was comforting to her to know the information that would cripple most adolescents simply, to some extent, amused her kids—though, my body was fighting between a laugh and a cry. "Mexico is probably closer and warmer."

Psychologists talk about the death of the parent, moments when they go from mom and dad to Shaughn and Marc or Debra and Steve. Taking them down from the pedestal of expectations to a level of humanity and reality. No one is perfect, and mistakes are made, sometimes often.

My father could deal with the matter at hand as his position at the fire department created some leverage. He was well respected, well known, and, most importantly, well liked. He was more intelligent than anyone gave him credit for. He always knew what role he had to play.

At that moment, there was no doubt it was the cards. Thin pieces of plastic with numbers, bank logos, and names that were not all the same, uprooting us again. My mom's face was tense with everything she had done and would continue to do for us. To give us the life she never had. The truth is that this world does not always hand you opportunities, and there will be times when you have to make your own. Billy Joel filled our four-wheeled traveling beacon as we headed for

Canada—a safe haven for my mother.

An hour into our disappearance, my phone began buzzing with my father's caller ID lighting up the screen. I looked to my mother for direction, and nodding, she said, "Answer it." We always knew the drill of when not to say the truth, not because my father couldn't hear it but because, odds are, he wasn't alone—our family's own secret code. "Mom took us on a vacation, and we will be home soon. Can't really talk, heading out; we love you." She drove until the weight of her eyelids far surpassed the weight on her shoulders.

19 December 2012

The following day was bright, and the car was cool with California's winter air. My sister spread out in the back seat, head tilted back, mouth open, surrounded by backpacks. My phone was just within arm's reach; maybe my dad had reached out again. Unaware she was awake, a quick flick of my mother's hand took it from me.

"No phones, baby. They ping the nearest cell phone tower every time they are turned on."

"Kinda feel like that is something you should have told

us yesterday." Laci was peeking up, always in a snippy, sleepy tone, even when completely sincere.

She wasn't wrong, but not like she didn't have enough on her plate. This was our first real day taking in everything that had happened in the past 24 hours. Fugitives, unshowered stiff muscles counting each cloud we passed on a road trip no one thought we would take. In reality, there's nothing of it, just doing what we're told.

Mcdonalds' was breakfast, and not complaining; a good breakfast burrito with a little bit of jam or honey makes it sweet. Pulling into a gas station for the third time, Laci had the bladder of a pea; there's always one person on every road trip making a fuss; not gonna lie, a little hobo shower in the sink to dilute my stench couldn't hurt. Puberty was starting to kick in, and my aroma had to resemble an overused sock for some reason.

You know that feeling when you are walking out of a shop, and you find yourself acting like you have to pretend you did not steal something even though you didn't steal anything? Eyes-catching eyes create an inexplicable amount of pressure. Well, a similar feeling was growing, but it wasn't because of a peanut butter cup shoved in my pocket; it was the fact that anyone passing by had the power to steal my mom away from me. You're probably thinking, why would you take a candy bar when there's already a warrant for your arrest? Well, I can't really say; I just wanted to taste it.

The bathroom had one small stall, a cracked mirror, and mould creeping up the sides of the wall. It was the first time my reflection faced me since we left. My hair grew tangled, and my mouth tasted of caked powder from the plaque building up. You really appreciate good hygiene when you lack the proper facilities to feel clean.

From the corner of my eye, my sister turned on her phone. She didn't seem bothered by the fact that she was caught directly disobeying our mother's orders. Not saying much, not just now, but in general.

As we returned to the car, the first thing said was a snitch's words: *"Laci used her phone."* Letting out a light laugh as she rolled down the window, drove about half a mile pretty fast, and threw one mobile device into bushes next one into a yard, she knew she didn't have the right to be angry. It was her fault we were in this position. *"You could have just taken out the sim cards."* Laughter really is the best medicine, even if you have to fake it a little. We were living out our season finale, and it was just one long punchline so far.

Every couple hours, we pulled over to pee, and when we did, mom would take something out of the back of the trunk, disappearing, and when she came back, whatever she was holding got left behind. It wasn't difficult to figure out what she was doing somewhere from California to the Oregon border; she did a whole lot of littering.

She could name every species of bird that flew overhead, and it wasn't really a game, just her showing off down the road for another 6 hours until we crossed a run-down little town with a name not worth mentioning. The little electric clock on the car radio read 2:04 a.m. as we pulled up behind a dusty orange storage container.

It reminds me of when my father received his fire chiefs badge and the journey we endeavoured just to be a part of it. Just a few hours into our road trip to San Francisco, it was just me, my mom, my sister, and a car that wouldn't start. That was the second time in my life my mom cried in my presence. Her head was bent over like a wilting flower. The colour drained from her face. We never have the best luck on the road.

When you're young, you don't understand the concept of weight; it's an overwhelming pressure that grounds you, only allowing yourself to see what is in front of you. To my mother, it wasn't just an engine that wouldn't turn over or strangers ignoring her plea for help; it was the loneliness and vulnerability that she had felt for her entire life that she had pushed down, so far down only to erupt at the odd hours of 3:00 a.m. in a dimly lit gas station—a woman without hope and two children. I can't help but wonder what she's feeling now. Fitting final thought for a long day before finally succumbing to a night of deep sleep.

The seams on the black leather interior smushed against my face, a growing pain stretching from where the baby hairs on my neck grew and down my spine caused by sleeping on a half declined seat, anchoring me into the present.

My mom's arm was still wrapped around me as she slept. Throughout the night, I'd feel her wake up and look around; it was in her moments when she thought she was alone that she let her fear show, startled by every passing car. Was it jail that we were running from or her leaving us with Dad? There are conversations we don't bring up, and her absence was one of them. Maybe we weren't running from anything but instead towards something else. All I could do was lie with her and in the hope of more.

The sun still lay below the horizon as the sky began to lighten to that sherbert blue colour, but the fear of where my thoughts would wander made being alone far less appealing. For now, it was funny, absurd, but also completely normal. To reside in this lack of conformity, chased by invisible men. Not ready yet for the moment it stops being funny. My mom kept us light, like the sherbert sky.

Nudging her out of a shallow slumber, my sister still asleep in the back, we took off from our hiding spot. Goodbye, orange tin can; thank you for the cover. The bags under my mother's eyes had darkened, and her hair fell brittle along her face. Rather than sit in the forefront of violent silence, my suggestion to turn on the radio was met with my mother's hands on top of mine, gesturing that silence was necessary, her cold, strained hand exposing blue popping veins. The days and her condition got worse, and today was not going to be a good day.

The gas tank had been running on empty for the past hour. The only person looking at it was me, though; I guess she didn't need to be reminded. Pulling into the lot, there was a cop parked in the coffee shop nearby, interrupting our conversation about how Laci peed in a cup at two in the morning and used one of my packed t-shirts as a sleeve. We were not a family of campers, so much so that it didn't even dawn on us to just pee outside. The cop wasn't doing anything threatening; he just existed and sipped his coffee, which was enough.

We passed the pump station. It didn't make sense why we would pass the pump station. Our big red beacon of a jeep slid into the spot between a beige minivan and a black truck—100 yards from me, my nameless nemesis in his pressed uniform.

My mother's broad shoulders lifted in a shrug, *"It is time to stop running; we have no money for gas or food or anything."* Thinking about that last sandwich sitting in my body and how they could have it back just to save a dollar for another mile of gas with my mom. We all knew what was coming and who was going. Our car, the big red beacon, stood tall, but mother stood taller.

We watched mother walk to the police car, and by the time the silver cuffs were on her, a crowd of observers had gathered. My face shoved into my sister's chest only barely stifled my tears; he needed to hear me cry and understand what he was doing. The weight of the red beacon shifted on its side as officer Gray, name tag catching the light, leaned against it. His mistake was opening the door for the anguish built up over the past two and half days; he let out in a spit-filled scream as close to his face as the law would allow me because even if you're a minor assaulting an officer is still a felony.

My sister held me tighter, forcing my eyes shut, but his eyes had to look into mine as if his actions were a choice. His back up had arrived, pulling into the parking lot that turned into a stage. Officer Gray looked at my sister, avoiding eye contact with me, *"Would you and your sister please get into the car."* He gripped my mother's arm and began escorting her to the back of this new arrivals police car.

"No." Yelling as if my words were above the law itself.

"Baby, look at me. Have I ever not come home." My mom's smile was soft as if she was proud of the strong, fierce girl she had raised. *"Will you please let my daughters stay in the car with me?"*

He looked as confused as the lady eating her sandwich

watching from the curb, almost as if this moment made him question the existence of his own authority, a soldier with orders following a blind law written by senseless men: his response, an open door to a caged cell on wheels. In the back of a police car, it's oddly cold, the metal absorbing all the heat, and there was a lot. He picked up the car walkie and spoke into an unseen realm. " I have Peta-Shaughn here with her daughters. She has turned herself in under the charges of absconding and wanted for questioning. We are on the road to CPS."

The building we approached was bleak and sturdy, and not long after arriving, my mother was taken elsewhere. There was no goodbye. She wiped my tears; she always hated crying, kissed me, and left. What do you say in a time like that? *I did it for us, I'd do it again, and I probably will.*

Child Protective Services was in big, bold letters at the top of a poster that held the only colour in a room filled with uninspiring walls and uninspired people. Wiry smiles ran across the faces of strangers; the lady at the desk, pitiful to our current situation, bought us Taco Bell. It was quiet for a long time. We got swivel chairs, though, and a big navy crewneck while waiting for our dad to arrive; that was all we knew how to do, wait.

Chapter Two

The Back and Forth

January 2013

She strutted through the house like it was a catwalk, 10 days she spent in jail. Convict of the year wearing this season's custom designer ankle monitor. Can being bad be hereditary if you love being bad the way she did, and if so, would she be the parent to pass it down?

The day was warm, with the sun heating up the windows. Scrolling through my laptop, looking up big houses for sale, homes hidden, lost on the mountain side, hopeful that we were on the same page, wanting to take on life with each other, to be the dynamic duo. My mom, the badass with her badass in training, escaped into a simpler life of luxury and adventure. We looked through dozens of houses, gasping at the uniqueness of each one and its various amenities. Movie theatres, gardens, saunas, and not one but three garages that we could turn into our own workshops and become the versions of the people we so desperately wanted to be. A month, that was it. A month until she would pack the car again and go for round two. This time alone.

"I'll follow you wherever you have to go so you won't go alone, Mom." A strong proclamation for an 11-year-old who'll soon turn 12.

My mom made life exciting in her way. When she set up for her new life, she cut off her ankle monitor, packed it up at all pretty and sent it back to the ones who put it on her. A classy fuck you to the those who thought the privacy of her whereabout was knowledge that belonged to anyone but her. Our bond, no one else could hold a candle to; how could we separate now?

A bad kind of excitement exists, usually involving caution signs, warning labels, and red flags going up everywhere. Parents protect you from that; no matter what may happen, it will always be okay. She had been in handcuffs, but now she was sitting back on her bed on her laptop, with me on my laptop next to her, our normal. If she weren't here in California, then California wouldn't be home. Though, after you run into a glass door, you approach the next one more cautiously.

She said everything with a laugh or smile and used

the exact quote so often that it burned into her brain. "*This too shall pass,*" A convincing statement to amplify that significance is short-lived, a creation of falsified importance to benefit the beholder. This did not pass, but it shifted something in all of us.

The night before my departure to Canada, bags packed, my father's eyes full. Saying goodbye was something he never intended to do at this age with me. He wasn't ready to let go, but it wasn't about him.

We all have a unique way of surviving in this world; at this age, one must love selfishly. Putting your hand in your own pocket.

A moment of love created me, and to understand how we love, we first interpret the love that brought us into this world. A tale of unforeseen circumstances that relish in the ideas of manipulation and greed are lined with moments of laughter and timeless shared looks. Before they were mom and dad, they were Shaughn and Marc.

So, to those who came from a love that stood strong and joyous till the end, embrace it; take it as it is one of the greatest gifts you will ever hope to have. They also showed me what it was like to watch love fade and be replaced with responsibilities. The first time my parents divorced, they stayed in the same house together and saw other people. Looking back, they probably should have stayed that way because the second time wasn't even a divorce. They walked away from each other in fits of rage and confusion. A scar was born.

Our tale of woe begins with Tracy, a young woman with family money but none of her own. She sought out a career in sales, as many people who begin to feel the weight of a dime in their pocket. She worked for an illustrious business woman with three kids, beautiful in stature, looks, and mind.

"On your trip, you have to meet my friend; he knows everybody and will take you out!" The boss, with kind words, cordially agreed to meet with the stranger.

On the last night of her trip away from home, amongst the tall buildings of San Francisco, she waited for a man with only a name, a contact, and an impatient hostess. Now this woman had a saying, 5 minutes early is on time, on time is late, and late is fired. This simple rule of thumb not only applied to her work life but also to the men she kept in close quarters. As she clicked her stiletto heels, the time in which they were supposed to finally make each other's acquaintance passed, only by a minute, until she caught the eyes of a man dressed head to toe in black. A turtleneck cusped just under his chin, a chin lightly covered in coarse black hairs, complementing the dark hair that sat atop his head, all reflected on his olive skin. His dark eyes stood out the most among all the darkness he encompassed himself in. It was only a moment of her adjusting the strap on her heel, shoes that nearly turned towards the direction she came, that instant her rule of thumb had met its exception.

Overlooking fisherman's wharf owned by the local Scarbosse family sat two unsuspecting individuals meeting for the first time. In the way the conservation flowed, the menus were left unattended and untouched. The bottles, however, ran like the Nile in spring; glass after glass, the two birds sang back and forth of the times before they were in each other's lives. Of the jobs they currently had and the heartbreaks they once felt. For the woman, she spoke of her children, the quiet, fearful daughter that slept in the hotel bed with her mother as she took another sip of her chianti, her boys that would most likely be playing World of Warcraft on the desktop right now even though they're not supposed to. For the man, he talked of his ambitions, the times he was confronted with death, and what it was like to hold life, a life with no attachment to his own yet managed to stay a part of him.

Hour after hour, the birds continued to chirp and search for a change of scenery, neither person aware of what they had started that day, only of where it was ending. Looking over the skyline of San Francisco at the prison of Alcatraz, their lips first met—an exchange of vows of imprisonment sealed in the long-forgotten kiss.

The following day as our beautiful maiden packed the limo towards the airport, she stopped by his work; dressed to the nines, she asked meekly where the man she met on the not-so-lonely night had gone. The news spread, like the wildfires the firefighters were meant to put out of a tall, beautiful woman in the firehouse looking for the man dressed in dark. To ensure their story didn't end that night, they confided in each other the uniqueness that lay in that day. Confirming that the kiss he leaves her with now shall not be the last.

The relationship between the two progressed at a speed comparable to an arranged marriage. Maybe it was fate who arranged these two, for he had let the word

I love you slip out over the phone within two weeks. For what seemed to be a fairytale of love so impatient, there is always a hiccup. An annoying recurrence that just won't seem to go away. The hiccup went by the name of Tracy, the bright-eyed employee.

On the third week after I love yous were exchanged, the woman finally had the time to catch up with her young employee, the messenger of fate.

Our woman held tight in her red corset and bought many bottles of gratitude for the messenger for a thank you she never got to say, for as the wine flowed between the two young women, loose lips leaked the lies that laid underneath her begotten fairytale. Tracy held the claim to our mystery man, *"He's my fiance, and we're getting married within the year."* Tracy's eyes were wider than ever at the words that escaped her mouth before she collapsed on the lap of our now very confused and hurt woman in red.

She took her home with her newfound knowledge contemplating the confrontation. The man she was about to pick up at the airport the next morning had hidden something from her that didn't sit right. How did this information stay hidden all these weeks? What kind of games were being played, and where did her piece fall on the board? As Tracy, now cozy in her bed waiting for the morning spins, our dear woman in red walked past the fireplace that once took hold of her home and lit it in flames. She thought of that day many years ago when she lost her last husband, the father of her youngest daughter, and wondered if she was cursed to walk the path of love alone. She thought back to her rule of thumb and thought maybe there were no exceptions, only mistakes.

But love does feed the famished and heal the wounded, and when it came time for our fellow birds to squawk, the winds carried their song away, he was forgiven and claimed her words untrue, and our lady had her prince charming again.

Meanwhile, he was preparing to pop the question, a silver ring from his beloved grandmother Mildred lay at the bottom of a pill bottle. Now our man was an old soul but young in heart. He knew to ask her children for their blessing. He had grown a love for them, and when he put that ring in the bottle, there was no future without them. The boys doubted not; having a firefighter with a big heart would be welcomed into their lives and home. The boys approached their mother with a bottle as our ever-so-eager man knelt on one knee. On February 27th, 1998, the family of three became a family of four, and on May 7th, two months passed, and a judge decreed it so.

Do you, Marc, take Shaughn to be your lawfully wedded wife in sickness and health, for rich or poor, for better or worse?

Do you Shaughn take Marc to be your lawfully wedded husband through sickness and in health, for rich or poor for better or worse?

They did. The following year that moment of just two strangers having dinner on Pier 37 turned into my birth. So you see, there was a time when he used to love how she would talk through movies and laugh too loud, and she loved how his smile ate his face and his music settled in the background. Now you can speculate on the intentions each one carried, but the outcome remains the same; my first introduction to what was love was fast and hopeless.

The tragedy in their love story was that love can also be blinding, and it is usually in these times when the fights grow louder before they fall to stilled silence.

Chapter Three

Gold

Vancouver, October 2013

The story about Goldilocks and the Three Bears is a solid contender for my favourite childhood story. Favouritism, a loose-lipped word for a tale that best exploits societies' need for "just right." Having melanin was right as long as there wasn't too much of it. Being stoic or loud or troubled was good. It adds to the individuality we all crave as long as we don't stray from the normal parameters. Oh no, that would be too much; it's an overbearing altruistic perspective unless you can make money off it. Then you're successful and wind up speaking to a lecture hall full of ill-informed 18-year-olds preparing to subject themselves to a lifetime of conformity. The porridge was never too hot or cold, nor was the bed too big or small. Goldilocks simply could not find comfort in her environment until it suited her needs. The prissy girl who messed up others' homes wasn't the connection drawn from the old tale; the porridge, the bed, and the things that adjusted to the comfort of others were my comparatives. Not to give off the impression that the times when spoken to my words were soft or right, but rarely in a way that would allow me to have my own comfort. To be my own Goldilocks.

My curls were straight from the moment I stepped out of the shower. The embodiment of my discomfort is my skincare routine, which includes ingredients with the word acid or brightener printed boldly. Not once did it occur to anyone that sending a ten-year-old girl to a school full of predominantly Caucasian students with 12-inch clip-in extensions would have a lasting effect on what was deemed beautiful. Coffee with a bit of cream, half white, half black, trying to figure out which side I'm supposed to like makes me loathe all of it; only a few hours before my flight, neatly stuffing as much of my identity into a suitcase again.

Six months—that's how long I lasted as Ty Ladas. A name as short as my patience for these shallow, coarse people. *Which penthouse is yours?* An assumption within a question stated by girls who were taught how to mask belittlement behind manners. The last word in every sentence dragged on longer than necessary and carried a high tone that gave new meaning to the term "white noise". This was supposed to be a building block in my relationship with my mother, but no one called the construction crew. She was different here, younger, rotating between bars, who knew her by name and drink. Usually around two in the morning on any given day of the week, if she wasn't home yet, I'd ring one of them, find her, and sit at the bar watching.

It was always men; I guess women in her line of work ran scarce. They lean in, and she would lean back. Her legs were always crossed, and the bill was always on her tab. She brings a drink every now and then to me, letting me order an endless supply of creme brulees. Who would they call to scold me for drinking, my mother, who sat a few feet away ordering for me? My presence was a reminder of how old she really was and yet a trophy of beauty for her to show off. I was a part of whatever image she was selling. I wonder if she even remembers it was my birthday.

Maybe she didn't know how often her lack of

presence struck me; only once did she hear me cry, a physical defeat and one that anybody could see. She had a rule: "If somebody is to see your weakness, let it be a worthy opponent." The promised mom and the love owed was an opponent that didn't exist.

My mother was not porridge; she owned her presence and chose her own side. She drinks vodka martinis and wears skin-tight clothing to show off her implants but a blazer to keep her classy. A modern-day Bond villainess with the bank to prove it. Though, this did not exempt her from insecurities. Not many people acknowledge how ironic the word insecurity is. To reside in security. It wasn't until she brought home a guy who was a bit too friendly with me that I left this place and her. I am not Marty Mcfly nor destined to save anyone but myself. She needed space, time alone to sort herself, and somewhere amidst the weekly flights, the urges started my own personal addiction.

Trichotillomania

My arrival back to California was intended to be a permanent one. My dad offered me the big room with a view of the magnolia tree, the sun outlining it now, my journal pressed into my fuzzy black blanket, with no noise. My fingers were distracted by a little bump on my head covered by hair.

My finger twisted around a single strand and uprooted it right down to the follicle, a release and a brief moment of pain, physical, confrontational. This thin little strand with a white bulb, a squishy translucent bead. My hands were removed from my consciousness, and I began pulling one strand after another. A knock at the door startled me out of my transfixed state.

Peace is like buying a ticket to the museum of your mind, passing by each exhibit, and observing what has remained in those still moments. Trying to be who you were in the mind of who you are now. *Behold the man I also know how to be.* To find solace in the past, we use words like forgiveness and acceptance to describe the steps to peace. The thing about museums, though, is the exhibitions change, damaged with time, collecting dust, and replaced, and for each one, we must sit back and take in what lies before us. Would mine be lit with a yellow hue like the sun or drowned in a brilliant white light like those in the hospital? Would my reflection see me tucked away, mirrored by the glass display? Maybe there could be interactive ones where you could push a button, and a countdown would flash on the screen in black and white, playing captured memories. This is why we call it peace of mind; otherwise, our mind falls to pieces.

Trichotillomania is an affliction of a variety of mental disorders, not a very common one. A unique form of OCD caused by stress or possibly hereditary and separately diagnosed as a body dysmorphic disorder. It seems that when we don't understand something, we try and cram in as many labels as possible, so if one of them is wrong, at least four others could be right.

I took four separate therapists on four separate occasions and a dermatologist to finally get to the breaking point of telling my father that it wasn't just some weird phenomenon of my hair falling out. That it was me ripping my hair out strand by strand every day, in every moment of silence. Thank god hats are trending because if I'm truly honest with myself, there was no desire to stop and, therefore, no intention of doing so, regardless of the damage it did. Though therapy was an interesting approach, repeating the answer to the same command " so tell me about yourself" turned my own identity into a virus. I would much prefer for someone to say " So why do you think you're so fucked up you need to pay someone to have an honest conversation." or " why do you surround yourself with people who are so incompetent that you feel a sincere conversation would scare them off and it is loneliness you fear more than that." The only real thing to come out amongst the ahas and mhms from Mr. I have a PhD in friendship number three, is that he recommends writing poetry. A ludicrous idea; luckily, those feel like home.

Sapling

She spoke of her heartbreak and countless ambitions

The fears that lay under every transition

She pleased and pleased even when she was alone

She was pleased with the image, the one she had grown

Even high in the sky on seats made of pleather

She cultivated the image of sun-shining weather

She wore false glasses that held no prescription

Only so that she may fit the description

She poked and prodded and beaten blue

Every version until shiny and new

She'll always be the more you are searching for

She'll coddle her love so that it won't be a chore

So hear her silent cries

And good intended lies

Listen closely and hear her

Then put down the mirror

Chapter Four

Deja Vu

*a feeling of having already
experienced the present situation*

8 December 2014

There was always this feeling growing up that, like I was destined for greatness, I suppose a lot of people must feel like this, though stunted by the idea of achieving happiness being their sole objective. Anyone can be happy, not everyone can be great or perhaps it is self endowed righteousness that will prevent me from being right. I was taught happiness is like a seashell floating on foam as long as you move with the current you won't drown.

The actions of others would further determine my fate as it happened again. Another day another parent faced man's authority, only this time, it was my father.

My father's coworker, Rubina, sat us down in the

living room. My heart goes out to her, she didn't sign up for my family's chaos, and here she was standing in the clearing next to the door as if to make a grand escape, but her maternal instincts gluing her to the grounds below, trying to be the pillow we could lay our head on in these times.

"Your dad..."

Laci cut her off, *"What happened?"* That is a fair question; he fought fires, for fucks sake, so to hear he had been arrested was honestly kind of a relief, the alternative being death. The words she spoke none of them made sense. How is it that my father, the stabiliser for our family, got caught up in the havoc, and does this mean we get to order dinner?

My sister could handle a lot regarding the hiccups of our mothers' job. You could even say she's unfazed by her extracurricular activities, although our father was a different story. As close as Laci could get to anyone, she got with him. You see, my sister is partially blind; maybe that's why she can't see out of rose-coloured glasses. She knew how to rely on herself but would lean on our dad when she couldn't. Her biological father died in a fire that ate the house before she was born. Regardless of the lack of his blood that flowed through her veins or his lack of contribution to her DNA, Marc was her father; Marc was all of our dads. My existence was just the one he genetically contributed to. Even my two older brothers who were deported back to Canada at the age of eighteen.

Rubina didn't stay long; there was nothing she could do, and she knew she could give no warm comfort as her presence was simply a reminder of our father's absence. For all that lay at our feet, none of it would take the day away.

My mother is an infection; to those good and bad, her last words might mean your last breath. Raw memories flooded, playing through my head like an old movie counting down.. 3, 2, 1..

An incident that lies in the fog of childhood, the moments we don't want to remember but can't seem to forget. That night the wine felt too sweet on my mother's lips and sour in her mind. She threw a glass of water on my dad and flicked the flour at my brothers. Maybe if she was met with tenderness, the night could have ended there. Maybe if someone just laughed with her, she could have gone to sleep feeling some sense of validation, but that wasn't the case. So it escalated to stories of men being locked in the back of trunks and left in the desert because you don't mess with whoever she decided to be at that time. Mumbling about the guns she had hidden and stacks of cash under the mattress that was far more comfortable than memory foam. My brothers sat with my sister and me in the bed my father built in the shape of a little house with pink and purple pastel stairs. We hid there while my mother drove the car over our bikes and through the garage door. Yes, you read that right, through it, still shut and after that very damaged, she disappeared maybe to find something that didn't exist and the next day we did as we always do when a situation stems from the happy-go-lucky lives we feel so obligated to live in, we pretend they don't exist.

To understand my mother, you have to understand her heart, for it is like no other. Imagine a castle made of spikes surrounded by wall after wall crafted in stone; around that lies a mote, and beyond that mote, a locked fence guarded. Now imagine everything that's built up around the beating vessel is transparent. A false expression bearing oneself as open-hearted. She wasn't some big bad wolf, though, coming to blow down everyone's house. She just likes shiny things. My dad does too. He prefers to swim in the reward than risk his righteous bearing, so it's better for someone else to do it. Lest we stain the image of the Ladas household, but here we are, stains and all. Though something didn't add up, like why was my mother charged with absconding me that day?

Marc opens and closes like a revolving door, holding back an emotional wrath. He was a man you could fall in love with in a day. He was Santa Claus, showed up just as often, and even had a big nose to match; the toys came in plastic, and in the security of knowing he was our normal taking us to cookouts, socialising, having friends, up until now.

My phone's buzzing brought me back to the world that was starting to feel like it fought against me. My friend was calling; we are 14. We don't call people; we text.

"Teaha, your dad is in the news." Her voice was quick like pistol Pete waiting to draw her weapon of mass diction.

The remote sat in sight as if to say be the star you always knew you were, Dad. She was right; there was his mug shot, pressed and rather pink in the face, not the best picture of him.

A swelling in my throat began, followed by blurry

vision, increased heart rate, and difficulty breathing, either developing a rapid respiratory infection or I'm about to cry. How unfortunate. They just came out, streaming in rivers of salt down my face without a care in the world, these wet rude inconveniences. Crying makes me uncomfortable, uneasy, and defensive, my mom's voice in the back of my head. You know those moments in movies where the person who's about to deliver bad news tells the other person *you're going to wanna sit down for this*, it's because when you're standing, you are already fighting against gravity, and now you have to fight against the weight of words, and that's a lot heavier. My friend is frantically on the other line, trying to calm me, as my crying voice sounds like a low-pitched yell. This is different; it's no longer a secret told in whispers. My mom's arrest was way more fun than this.

My sister came in, wrapping herself around me as gravity pulled me down. There we sat on the black carpet of my room with the television projecting my father's face and a faint voice on the other line. Holding me until my momentary rock began to crack too, and there we sat where it didn't matter whether my top was hers or not, though it was, or any cliche sister fight because, on this black carpet, we melted until the sunset.

The Following Day

The magnolia tree was an overgrown bucket of water when the rain fell. Its leaves would pool, and the warm water would weigh down the unexpecting pads.

The fence that divided the front from the back, the exposed from the hidden, smothered in the night, carried my weight as my legs swung back and forth in anticipation of his arrival. Rubina had messaged, saying he was on his way home. What should I say? How was the food? Make any friends? Drop the soap? His car pulled into sight, and the bags under his eyes carried heavy thoughts. His eyes caught mine as the ground caught my feet. What the hell? Who is this man? His eyes felt hollow and yet full of anguish.

"Are you gonna divorce Mom" *shit*, definitely not the right thing to say.

His lips parted, and no words greeted my question; maybe bringing her up right now wasn't the best time. What do you say when you find yourself on the edge staring down a great fall, feeling yourself slipping into it?

Everyone wanted to hear a story of a man who was thwarted by a conniving monster, who absconded with her children and fled the country. Sorry to disappoint, but the truth is far less over the top. Yes, she fled the country, a country that didn't want her, proven by the many failed deportation attempts. In a world like ours, you must understand the differences between acting and reacting. When you act, you create a new path; reacting follows the one you're already on.

As the newspapers began popping up everywhere and the television screens lit up with the faces of the people who brought me into this world, word quickly spread.

Forcing talks between teachers, some of whom already believed they knew exactly who my family was, greedy animals that lurked in the night. Hiding our hooves and horns under jackets and hats, a dark robin hood stealing from the poor to fill their forever unsatisfied pockets. You can imagine the countless pitiful doe eyes that failed to spark anything in me other than resentment towards a person's inability to mind their own fucking business.

My favourite, though, had to be Miss Rorchbach. My history teacher, with a long southern drawl, was more of a companion. She would blatantly tease us about our faults and had more movies about pearl harbour or some famous battles than Ben Affleck; my attendance was nothing short of barely passing; my grades, however, reflected a much more studious person, so she accepted me, with the occasional talks of *"if you just applied yourself a little more Teaha you could run this world."* This day was different; no, on this day, the folded newspaper on her desk reflected my family's not-so-private life, *"sorry, I don't have the homework for today. Yesterday was eventful, and judging by the newspaper on your desk, you can already guess why."* She is not a silent woman, but she asks only one question at this moment. *"Who are they to you?"* My response was a simple remark cutting the conversation short. *"My parents."* More thrown off by my smile saying it than the fact itself, she excused my missing homework. It's sadistic how much enjoyment was received from watching people tune into my life, excusing every obligation.

Some people hold onto shock like it is the purpose of life to be traumatised. This is developed through the fear of what may be next. It's easy to get caught up and feed into our daily doubts, but true prosperity is forged with an iron blade that can cut through unnecessary quips and build on the vices that allow us to stand above it. Youth trauma is a recipe for character development; one cup of adaptation, a teaspoon of ego, and a pinch of sugar reveals just enough of an open wound to feed the pity and, in turn, allows for an extension on all final projects, assignments, and homework. For the right teacher, you might even get out of an exam.

That was the only thing my father said this morning. Broken eyes and limp words. *"Use this monkey."*

Everyone likes to ask *what they did* like they weren't already speculating from what those gaudy newspapers had written. *How are you feeling?* There are feelings, just not happy ones, but this isn't my first rodeo bitch; the Bulls just got a different rider. How do you express that to people? No one wants to hear that you are not doing great. They want to see the smile and hear the drama so they can bring it home and to the lunch tables, and honestly, Mom and her associates would take care of me if necessary. My father was a grown man who seemed pretty convinced he would walk away from this. So, just more waiting.

Drifting around friend groups was easy in a school this big; people came in a variety pack, but when the prolonged social gatherings formed on this day, it was as if someone rang a bell, and everyone became my closest friend, close enough to ask me about it. My sister took all this like a bad hangover, kept her head down, and focused on her studies. My mother has been silent for most of this situation, organising and meticulously calculating the various outcomes, while my father began to get angry, smiling less and swearing more.

Like most days when you're a high schooler in California, you end the eight-hour school torment by getting high with your friends; the joint we had lit turned to ash, and we sat in comfortable silence. Today's drama ended, and the lunchtime discussions would revert to poorly imitated Dave Chapell skits tomorrow. The progression is inevitable because as much as we say we care about other people's problems, we don't like to hear about it twice.

It was a civil war, and the civilian casualties came down to just one. My mother's version of taking care of something was having us smuggle cash back to California to my dad in cute little envelopes. If money created the problem makes sense; it might solve it too. An odd age to learn the semantics of border law; you cannot travel with more than 9,999 dollars US without declaring it, to declare something means a written record will be taken for referral, and the statute of limitations is a deadline created to determine if someone can be charged, fraud, well that one kind of explains itself, and tax evasion is a felony. Maybe, this is my training to be the world's greatest lawyer. Not a bad origin story, the Batman of Law.

My dad didn't fall into the bottom of a bottle, but on the rare occasion he let himself go a little too far, the curtains of composure toppled, and he would speak of his disdain for his loss. Understandably, he was facing losing everything he had built, and he was accomplished; award ceremonies were held to pin a shiny button on his chest, and people attended just to watch and not just anyone; politicians and journalists. His rebuttal towards his situation was that he knew nothing, just as shocked as everybody else. Regardless of who a person is to you, love is only as blind as choosing not to see and how much he does not see. We had A Lincoln Navigator, a BMW M6 in a rich custom yellow, and fancy trips in big houses; it wasn't a mystery that we lived shiny, or maybe it's just easy to ignore when you only come home on the weekends.

He sat at the foot of the oak table my grandparents had given us. Running his fingers along a water stain that had marked the wood. He had a kind of crazy laugh when he got angry, the one that makes your own face scrunch up in distaste. Sometimes all you can do is laugh so you don't cry, but when he spoke about the potential severity of the case, he looked like he wanted to burn the whole world down and dance in gas-lit rain. You have to imagine the kind of person you have to be to be a firefighter or paramedic and work for S.W.A.T. You have to go through life with a hollow logical stare, almost void of human attachment.

Trials are never short, it's a strenuous waiting game, and unlike my mother, he was determined to see it through, So we carried on. The option was always there, though. Sell the house, run away, be a family, and remove the individualism created only when there is problem after problem.

Chapter Five

The Last Straw

Four months later

My dad once told me that when it rains, and the water lands on a duck, it doesn't get absorbed or even bother the duck; it just falls off. This is because the duck's feathers are hydrophobic, and sometimes in life, rain pours down, and the sun is hidden, so the duck has to sit and wait for the rain to stop. Letting each drop simply roll off its back.

My parents spoke to each other less and less; my absence at home was expected, out with my friends, making mistakes. Ignoring as much of life as someone can.

Half past noon and the weather was timid. Our boys, people who often occupied our lives daily, were on their way over with bud (marijuana, the word bud is friendlier, sounds like you're calling someone you just had a big fight with). Apple had curly hair and didn't hate it; she picked the music while my face was neck-deep in the fridge. Some blackberries were hidden in the back when she put on my favourite song by Shirley Bassey—a conquistador when she was in her prime in the music industry. Highly recommend listening to it.

We burst out in an off-key duet, singing, *"HEY, BIG SPENDER BA DA DA DAAAA! COME ON AND SPEND A LITTLE TIME WITH MEE!"*

Authentically submersed in vulgarity in her words and the way she carried herself. My flaw, always saying yes as the idea of embodying someone powerful was too intriguing to pass, regardless of the consequences that had never been severe enough for me to know you don't walk away from everything.

The doorbell rang, interrupting our America lacks talent audition; our boys were here.

Pulling up chairs around the table outside, laying out their various grinders, papers, and of course, backwoods. Daniel and Apple were going back and forth about the music. Daniel wanted to play some rapper whose name starts with lil. Occupied by maintaining the balance of my chair, when you say something, you could potentially say the wrong thing; weed makes me paranoid.

A big bottle of crystal clear Swedish vodka makes its appearance.

"Mmmm... das is very, very nice," is a German accent for a Swedish drink; as far as people know here, all foreign is the same foreign.

In the kitchen, where most people keep their glasses, a knot began to grow in my stomach, my heartbeat was too apparent, and my words muffled thanks to the glamour of cottonmouth, high tendencies.

A dirty glass, just slightly contaminated. Rubbing off a small smudge, fixating on this little imperfection, this blur on an otherwise clear glass. It's just starting to disap-

"What are you doing? Come on; I'll help with those."

Apple grabbed three of the glasses, one of which contained the smudge.

Hand to hand, the blunt was passed around, the object of attraction—the common denominator. The boys made jokes about what they would do to our maths teacher with the big breasts and how J. Cole was the only one who understood them. They accepted my timid traits and didn't make me feel less for it. How could you not love someone for that, my company, to sweeten the misery of home?

Today Ended An Hour Ago

This was a day of firsts, the first time being laid down on a countertop limp while others pulled down my pants, the first time someone had taken coke off my ass and then proceeded to flip me over and do lines off my unsuspecting breasts. Every spin, turn and yank of clothing is harder than the next. If not for the booze and mental pacer fitness test of a drug, would I have been so willing to get on the table? Apple did it first, and hell, if your friends jumped off a bridge, would you do it too? Were the little jerks of my hand pulling away my body, trying to run to someplace other than where it currently resided, on this cold, unforgiving counter where I once sat and had cups of coffee with Apple's mom the morning after a wholesome girly sleepover? Wholesome might be an overstep as most nights we still smoked from her colourful pipe or took shrooms and watched Coraline and plotted ways to escape to some empty house, undisclosed soundproof basement, or hell, even the elementary school up the road with a flat rooftop. Yay. a nickname for a word that did not correlate to the reaction of its presence. Yay, snow, blow, cocaine white fluff in one nostril followed by the other.

Within these few hours of privileged freedom, the house was filled with bottles, boys, and bad decisions.

The berating conversations that were too loud for a too-bright day, the sliding door displaying my statue of stability, my weight heavier than usual.

Time passed at an immeasurable rate since that first sip of alcohol graced my lips; I was on Apple's bed; I wanted to be here, just not sure how I got here, but here is where I am. A boy was standing at the foot of the bed, my legs hanging over, coughing out a laugh that clawed out of me. His hands ran up my legs, applying pressure to my thigh. Did I bring him here? His face is close to mine, his legs intertwining with mine, his movements forcing mine. Did I want this? The bed sheets curled around my toes in shame. Then all of a sudden, everything went dark.

Pressed against Apple's parents' bed, completely unclothed. A sharp pain crawled up the side of my legs into my stomach. He was still here, with me. Maybe if I thought of the sounds of fireworks, that's what this could turn into; it didn't. The room fell and rebuilt, spinning; he stopped just long enough for my feet to find the ground and my hands to steady the edge of the bed. Ten steps to the bathroom; I counted. In the mirror, he was in the midst of the collapsing room behind me, a shifting blur of blue eyes emptying, slowly getting bigger. The weight of him grabbing my bare waist threw me into the shower. My head greeted the wall hard enough to induce a blackout.

A bright white hue and dusted shadows creeping on the ceiling stared back at me, the door was open, and he stood in the frame. Our eyes caught just before he walked out. My back was still firmly pressed against the floor, numb and cold all at once. My mother raised me stronger than this, louder than silence; if you are somewhere you don't want to be, move. Exposed and humiliated, contorted by abuse.

One foot in front of the other, soon you'll be walking out the door. A song from a Christmas movie, a strange thought at a time like this. Simple and repetitive, and an achievable goal. Partially present in the hallway. Twelve steps roughly, eyes open dead ahead, just walk.

Men's voices were drowning in gravel. *"Woah, you are naked,"* an observant friend of a friend; at this point, all attendees were unbeknownst to me, or maybe it was a ghost.

Jeans on the floor, my shirt crumpled up on the bed, the cotton filling the empty space of my palm. Shirt on, naked no more, worn out, and a little torn. A bruise on my thigh and a little bump on my head.

Don't think, don't think, don't think... but if the thoughts stop, all that's left to do is feel. Dreaming of a peaceful place on the beach, waves crashing, counting the seconds - the pull, the build, and the release. Imagine every detail, the sand tumbling amongst the white water, then count. one…two…three…four crashes, again. one…two...three… crash, again. Interrupted by the sound of the door refusing to remain shut. Don't look; you don't want to, fuck, more drowning voices and unrecognizable faces.

Sober the fuck up, please. Sheets could not shield me, nor my tightly tucked knees could prevent his hand from exploring; black spots began to grow like weeds in my visions. The screams in my head came out as little more than a whisper: goodnight, men who stumbled in one after the other. Don't be there when my system restarts.

A boulder on my chest, but it wasn't a boulder; it was a man. They decided to stay. He had buried himself in my neck and his finger, his fucking fingers causing an unbearable amount of pain wriggling inside me, swollen, tender to the touch. The spins, spinnier than ever, as my shoulder lurched into his chest, retreating him up and off of me wearing this awful shit-eating grin like he did me a favour, my lips still wet. Two men sat in the chairs in the corner like they paid good money to see a show. His hand grabbed my shoulder, pinning me down, until Daniel burst through the doors, talking about messing up one of the motorcycles, capable of nothing more than staring, at the bed that stole my clarity, a body that no longer felt like my own and the men who stripped it all away.

Daniel busted in; you're late, superman.

He spoke to a drunk hooker in an old Tarintino movie, a lifeless extra.

"*Ders.*"

It must be the man still resting on top of me, an unfinished name for an unfinished fella. Daniel grabbed my shoulders and spun up consciousness with a light shake. He said something about Apple.

Words left my mouth but held no possession.

"*Shit! It's 5:15.*" Before I even made it to a fully upright position, they were gone, and I was alone. Everyone was buzzing around, trying to figure out where to go and what to do; the scratching of chairs being pushed, a roar of men in a brothel, and this room now stained with my ghost and blood. The imprint of my nails marked my palms. Where was Apple?

My breath couldn't escape me; if the oxygen didn't leave me, maybe time would stand still. Okay, One foot over the bed, good, now the other, a wind-up toy with no one to turn the key but me. Self-reliance is a bitch. Little by little, then all at once, my feet lead me towards my crushed garments. Thank god my phone is shoved into my back pocket, a safety net. Siri, I command thee, call Father.

"*Yello*" He always answered the phone like he just got some great news.

Usually, my response consisted of colour because his hello sounds like yellow. I couldn't muster that up right now, "*pick me up, please.*"

"*I will be there in 15.*" Thank god he picked up.

Okay, okay. My new objective, remove myself from bed, leave the room, and find Apple. The door was still wide open as if it was just locked, unwavering thoughts aside and moving forward.

Warning signs alarmed me as my stomach began to feel like the early stages of an eruption were beginning. My bambi legs carried me back into that bathroom because it was no longer just any bathroom; it was that bathroom. Emptying all the contents inside of me took three solid, hefty heaves. My movements on autopilot towards the main door, and there she was, revealing the bruises on her leg from the man who pinned her down. Today needs to end.

This was America's land of free; take what you can, give nothing back. To act in accordance with the laws of others is to be an outlier in your life. At this moment, we were outliers who were laid out, guided by wreckage left in my wake.

She tidied up the piles of beer cans and glass bottles towering together on the table while the sun lay on my face and my ears filled with the sounds of my father's radio growing nearer.

"How are you feeling, Tea?" Disappointed was a look rarely seen upon my dad's face, but now, in this hour, as the words slurred out and my breath drowned in liquor, he couldn't help but feel his own defeat.

My eyes closed, slumped against another cold plain; winter makes everything cold. "Just feel sick."

Stumbling subtly intoxicated on the journey from car to bed, making the mistake of trying to pick up a rock that looked like Elvis's hair on the way, and clinging to my bed; the sun hadn't even set yet, and when my eyes shut, the day will be over.

Tuesday, maybe, it's black outside; time keeps going. The spins from yesterday must have just been the alcohol because what was racing around my head now was violent and out for revenge—existing solely between the space of not awake and not asleep for hours until the day forced its progression through hygiene routines and pains of hunger.

After a delicious cup of water and toasted water with a side of water for breakfast, my dad sat with me on the couch, a consoling arm wrapping me. Olivia's mom had called him, and they had gone to the police and the hospital. A rational thing to do. He wanted me to talk with no words to say. With no feelings to be felt, all that remains is the graphic details and a description of my perpetrators.

"There's nothing to say to the police, and I will tell them that. Can you take me to the store? I need to pick up the day-after pill, and then I don't want to talk about it again. I am fine." Was it my responsibility to console or conceal?

The police on the other line spoke as if this call had been made a 100 times over, *"Good morning Miss Ladas; we have a report here filed on behalf of Apple Callwell regarding a sexual assault; she is currently in the hospital having a rape kit done…"*

"Thank you for calling; however, I wish to abstain from any claims."

This is where being the daughter of those who tussle with the law has its limits. My voice silenced as incorporating any police into the matter would surely fall alongside my father's mugshot in the next daily news-press. After what happened, we were no longer a family, just strangers living in the same base. We didn't talk about that and weren't talking about this.

My dad called my mom, and my mom called me. " Do you want me to handle this?" A life or two in my hands are as heavy as a nine millimetre; if I had said yes, it would have been done within the week, and there would be one less piece of trash polluting this planet, but what about his mom? The one who worked at the Apple store in town, she would have to come home to a quiet house every day and pack up the boards we used to spray paint outside in their backyard.

"Thou shalt not kill mommy. I can handle this, and I love you."

"And I shant, my darling. I love you too." Could hear her as sick as a parrot.

"Can I come home for a bit?"

Without hesitation, *"Of course."*

After a few days with her living in a different penthouse than the one we had before, shopping and dinners at the tea house dressed in heels and pressed white dresses. That day temporarily ceased to be for me, and it was foolish of me to think others would do the same.

Five days later, right back in his house again, coloured cans to the side, and the first topic of conversation that day was the day no one but I wanted to forget. Oz wouldn't look me in the eyes. I left his house and a school that did not value its students as anything but a reputation—gone for good this time. The whole continent was tainted. Take some time for myself, meet the cheerleader with a solid GPA thanks to Adderall and Google, the end of week high flight risk who turned into a high school dropout whose name will be as forgotten as that same Monday night or maybe not, considering new articles would frenzy every time there was an update in the case.

The tunnel is supposed to have a light at the end of it, and somehow it will all just work itself out one way or another. There's a part that people seem to miss when making such a profound statement; it is that the symbolic light is a representation of a brighter future. However, that light is also a representation of death. If no light is found in this lifetime, there will be the sweet relief of not having to live another day in it. Our supposable God will then hold us and tell us, "*You did good, hun; you gave it your best.*" Or, depending on the religion, you go to hell for committing such an act. God has the darkest humour of all if he or she is the one kicking it at the end of the line sipping gin. I guess the only thing I ask when my time comes is to not let my death be painful for it to be the last thing I will experience for the first time and there is a beauty in that that shan't be overshadowed.

My dad, sitting around the same wooden table that always stayed there, me coming home from friends who were as friendly as the cactuses in Arizona. The same smells and magnolia trees caving to the rainfall, making a mess of the yard.

My online school ended in May, and neither of us really knew what to do with me. He talked about me moving back to California to attend a middle college for two years, and then it would jumpstart my education. We even took a tour of the school after retreating to the same drowning cactuses. My blood wasn't clean nor poisoned upon my return home. Pulling the car into the driveway and opening the big gate where my legs used to swing down above the rubble path, straight through the kitchen into my father's room. His heart condition was a limitation for him but an opportunity for me. His medication was concealed, the lid was childproof, and apparently, I'm still a child because that thing is hard as fuck to get off, but it did, it opened and pouring about seven or eight pills in my hand and popping them into my mouth like a jolly rancher alleviated the stressors of tomorrow and every day after. Then to the kitchen to put my face in the sink adding some water to the dry mix. I was organised as if someone had left me instructions. The white powder left on my hands reflected a matte white in the light emitted from the windows and coated in snow as if to remind me why this was enticing.

My back is pressed against my wooden headboard, and the leaves are wrestling outside. Grandpa's dog stretched out by the pool; my heart was the loudest thing in the room. My hand warmed the back of my neck and ran my fingers through my hair to feel every little patch missing. Mom would be fine because she always had enough going on; my dad might just receive some sympathy points for losing his job, losing his daughter, and my sister's life would hardly change as she would graduate this year and leave everyone behind anyway. Then my reflection sat with me; though her background was different, she was anywhere but here wearing a smile that lingered after a laugh, her face held time and sun-kissed cheeks, looking fascinated by the things she had never done, freed from the misery of fatalism. How are we to meet if tomorrow never comes?

Two fingers stiff, invading as far back into my mouth as possible to smack that hanging fleshy teardrop. Coughing until my decision was flushed away, the remnants only slightly dissolved. Sometimes the clock is irrelevant, and you have to decide when the day is over and sleep so you don't live life backwards.

Chapter Six

The World Belongs to the Brave

5 August 2015

"*You know why you won't die? Because God's afraid of me.*" A beautiful final quote from my mother before my flight boarded. We talked about religion a lot in our family. She says God speaks to her, and I say there's medication for that. Through every conversation, we negate the idea that anyone is right or wrong about religion, for it is impossible to be so stubborn to believe that anything is not possible, but if there is a God, wouldn't he hate religion for its inability to consolidate and unify the very people He (or she or it) created for thousands of years.

"*The sin of gluttony is when we stuff ourselves so much that we feel sick. There need not be somebody to tell you, you feel sick to feel the weight of sickness itself.*" This is a beautiful quote by me reprimanding those with a holier-than-thou personality; we spoke about the big sins a lot. Typically, thou shalt not steal, end the conversation, or turn it into a fight. I will miss them, but neither my mom nor dad were situated in places best for me, so option number three is to run far, far away where my cheeks may kiss the sun, both of them.

When you look at the sea from above, it's stagnant like sand, untouched by wind, with Highway to Hell playing in the background. Headphones are single-handedly the greatest invention of the 21st century. The ability to remove all sensations and replace them with a repetitive pattern that could take over your thoughts like a growing weed is sensational. In music, be it rock and roll or jazz, you can get lost in the imagery the sounds create. The electric guitarist slides his fingers down the string, its vibration a sensation that radiates its own translation of cords. Painting a picture so chaotic that you can't help but feel the movements to interpret it. A combination of being 35,000 feet in the air and listening to Bon Scott transports the mind into a different dimension with visuals in overdrive, and a good feeling was blooming inside me. Grow little saplings, grow.

In scuba diving, the only way to achieve balance is to control your breathing. A controlled breath means that you are stabilised. Stable is foreign to me in context by now, after living in over 11 different houses and hotels, attending over six different schools, never actually graduating from any of them, and adjusting year by year. Now here I am, standing on the soil of Fiji alone, kind of. I've joined a volunteer project abroad for certified but inexperienced divers to embrace that instability and make it mine.

The air was congested, with the sun reaching every corner of the sky. The weariness of the flight had washed away and was being replaced with an indescribable newness. After 14 dull wasting hours in the sky, there was a three-hour bus ride on the island known as Viti Levu. It was worth it for that moment when it would peer over the land with the sun kissing the horizon line and the crisp blue waters of the ocean. Marvellous. The sea brought out my extrovert because how could you not alert everyone in the vicinity to look in awe? Three months—that's how long my time away was initially set for. My instructions were to get off at Pacific Harbour, a clean and colourful place with restaurants lined around a big pond and palm trees creating shade over the patios. A man, Ron, should be waiting for me.

He approached with a big smile and wide eyes. *Bula*, Fijian, for hello. The word's meaning goes much deeper; it means my life welcomes yours. Supposedly, the language is deeply rooted in the communities, despite English attempts. "Bula, sir", he introduced himself and who he was to the project, more specifically, that if any mischief came about in my stay here, he would be the one to answer to, understanding that a minor in his care couldn't get into any trouble. My mother must have warned him. The drinking age in Fiji is 18, just two years shy.

Half of all the volunteers were eating lunch on the balcony that mirrored the kitchen, while the other half were off on an afternoon dive, tasting salt water. They brought my luggage to my room for me because they had been waiting to do my introduction with another volunteer who had arrived before me. His name was Luitpold, a German boy who was also staying for three months. He gave me a cheeky grin. Having never met a German from Germany before, I wasn't sure how to approach him. Don't they do kisses on the cheek or a salute? An ignorance befitting my stifling lack of culture. I figured there would be a lot to figure out today.

He was 20 but looked no more than 17. Contemplating how much of myself to reveal, the three of us sat in his office, reviewing schedules and housing. There are 34 beds and six units; all units are co-ed and equipped with a kitchen and seating.

"As long as you know your limits and everyone is safe, you can have a good night. There's a hotel bar most head to at night called Uprising, and it's closer than where I picked you up from. Nothing but a five-minute walk from here." His English was good, but his accent was a muddled-up combination of all the international volunteers teaching him different words. We were given work shirts and sarongs that we would wear when we travelled to different villages to teach kids or paint/construct schools. Attire for diving, collecting data, doing species counts, tagging hammerheads, or planting mangroves was based on what we felt comfortable in. Considering I'm sitting in this chair wearing eyelash extensions and a fresh acrylic manicure, I didn't exactly plan for so much mud, but making a good first impression comes in two parts: the first thing they see and the first thing you say.

My only obligation today is to eat, socialise, find the biggest herd of people, and figure out how to summarise my identity in a good three sentences. Pick three topics of conversation to talk about after you say your name and where you're from, then excuse yourself so the jury has a minute to deliberate their verdict on whether you are cool, nerdy, shy, funny, or an outcast.

Approaching the herd, there was an immediate bombardment of extroverted boys attempting to guess my origin based on my name; it was a rather cute icebreaker. " We thought you had to be from Russia, Germany, or Italy, but now maybe Spain or Brazil." The excitement was warming, like a group of misfits all fit for each other. The girls were quieter, which made me more cautious, most likely because it was most of their last night here. This wasn't high school, and thank God for that.

Just a girl from California—that was my simple story. They made jokes about me being the youngest, as if being 23 years old meant you walked with a cane or needed a new hip. The oldest recruit was a man in his forties. Age doesn't really mean you stop running from something or towards something else.

A pack of Marlboro Gold was stuffed in my backpack; it's a handy crutch in a new place. I could smoke three or four in a row and never touch them again; I guess my addictive parts did not extend to tobacco. Luit was outside smoking; it was nice to be new to someone.

He sat on the porch before the rooms, looking at the sky. A plastic cup, ironically placed in the centre of the table. Holding it in my hands, I said, "On Wednesdays, we pick up plastic." Using the butt to burn a smiley face into it and sticking my cigarette inside the line of the mouth. "Aha, like the mean girls quote and our schedule, you're a funny girl," he said, waving his finger at me. Others joined, and these were my people for the next three months.

Running from the western winds. We are driven here by first-world problems. Most of the volunteers were from European countries that only felt real when you read about them. The staff and the propagule nursery were the only things consistent about this place, but even those seeds had to be planted eventually.

A kava ceremony was scribbled into tonight's schedule; apparently, we would not be sipping on champagne but on a mixture that resembled dirty water, an anaesthetic that left the tongue feeling numb. Everyone got ready in the main hall. The women dressed in grass skirts wore red lipstick and wrapped tribal cloth into bandeaus. "Yall do this a lot?" Talking to the people who were leaving soon meant any wrong impressions would go with them. "Only once every few months, you came on a good day."

The sun hadn't even set yet, and the event was going into full swing. The chef and maids here were locals, bossy ladies who reminded me of my aunties in Jamaica—gripping our heads to apply facial markings and red lipstick. Lining us up so we could learn traditional dance steps, the movements were concise but fluid. A lot of the girls here were English, and I'm not saying they can't dance, but if you ever see a stick bend to a breeze, there's not much give.

A chief had come to conduct the ceremony, and we had all gathered sitting in a circle; for the first time, everyone was in view. There were about 12 of us. He sat quietly in the centre, grounding the root into the coconut milk. His voice was slow and steady as he spoke. "Traditionally, the woman chews the roots and mixes it, but that has been lost. The kava root is meant to heal the wounds we have on the outside and inside. When you drink from this, your healing begins, tying us all to this bowl, to this tribe." He drank it and handed it to the first person he saw, me. "Clap your hands and say Bula drink, then clap three times more." The liquid tasted like the grass it grew in, numbing my mouth. As it was passed around, it wasn't a high feeling that took over; just joy. Unable to be anxious, if this is what anaesthetics feel like, then let it rain kava in California.

The cook handed me a machete to cut down some palms for mats; no one had ever handed me a big-ass knife before, and my mother wouldn't even let me use a turkey carver on Thanksgiving. Lutpold and another guy came with me around the front, holding down palms and cutting one after the other. While others cooked the cassava root in the ground or grilled the meat.

We ate together as the sun set and fire dancers lit up the sky. When they stomped, the ground awoke and pushed back. After the professionals had set the bar, the volunteers turned to do the dancing. The men went first, performing what they had been shown just hours before. The only light emitted was from the torches. We didn't have neighbours to disrupt. The music was so loud it echoed through the trees; if the trees had ears, the elders would plug them, and the children would dance.

The boys fumbled and smiled as they danced and beat their chests. Primal animals are being released from their cages. Impressively, after only an hour of practice, they took to it. It could teach the cheer team a thing or two. Bending backwards with one hand on the ground and the other in the air, thrusting their hips forward. Everyone was hollering and whistling as the grass skirts flipped up and down. It was effortlessly carnal. Lighting up like plankton at night and only glowing when disturbed. This was our initiation, day one. By the end of it, we were feeling fully prepared for someone to tell me to sign away my firstborn child. If this was a cult, they could have me, and we haven't even been diving yet.

My nerves had made me scrutinous of the day and cynical of the people. You figure if you keep the bar low, you won't get hurt by expectations. There are a lot of tendencies that need to be unlearned, so to the child whose smile ate her face and whose laughter filled the room, I miss you and will find you again, reminding myself that as long as she is remembered, she is not too far away.

1 November 2016

My accommodation, dive gear, and food were all prepaid for by my mother. We spoke once every other week, a conversation never lasting longer than a hot tea staying hot. Returning to a part of who we once were the moment we picked up the phone.

Almost three months had passed like nothing, diving every other day. Going to local schools and villages to paint, build and teach. When my mother answered the phone this time, it was me begging for an extension. What was there to come back to? "You can't hide out in Fiji forever, Tea." She was right, "But I can for four more months if you'll let me." She didn't say no very often if she had the means. Though homelessness in Fiji could be worse, she said yes.

Looking at my bag, next to it my fins, mask, and hair brush, "Hey, Luit, do you have a lighter, and do we need to bring our dive cert cards?" He popped his head into my room and threw a lighter at me. "No, and we're leaving in 15, so hurry up." Shit, stuffing my things into my dry suit bag, my wet swimsuit clinging to my shirt at a quarter to seven in the morning. Last one to arrive as usual at the pick-up site, our front door. The boat to Beqa left after 10 o'clock, and it was a longer trip than our normal dive site boat ride because the boat really wasn't a boat but a dinghy. A term for floating tin can with an engine. Tiger shark sightings became increasingly frequent, and this island's crew had the best spots. Blew my allowance, but entirely worth it.

After arriving and checking into the empty resort, we boarded the dive boat. The six of us huddled together in excitement as they debriefed the dive. The water was chummed thick, far more than anyone would deem safe. About 10 of us were in the water, the six of us behind the rock wall, two feeders in front adding more and more chum until visibility was close to none and two behind with metal prongs just in case. There are two dives; each is about 30 minutes, with tank change in between. Fairly standard for a shark dive. The first 10 minutes were silent, with the occasional black tip or bull coming around. Then, she was a four-and-a-half-metre tiger shark holding back no curiosity and swimming right up to the wall where every diver was leaning over to get as close as possible. A row of hands reached up, grazing the sandpaper skin. Screaming into your regulator sounds a lot like someone getting tortured in a movie, but none of us could help it. So much so that it took several minutes to realise a sea snake had wrapped itself around my fin. On the surface, where the sea meets the sky, BCDs were inflated with enthusiastic incoherent words, and after tea, cookies and a cigarette, we did it all over again.

Diving with sharks feels like a hallucination. Every second in the water pulls you into a realm that looks quiet and empty from above but, in reality, is teaming with life.

We returned, had dinner and drinks and headed home the next day. For lunch, we all went out to a restaurant in town. Even though Fiji doesn't exactly have soup weather, there was this soup that was one of the best dishes. Accompanied by a vodka soda, and that was one of the last things I remember.

Destroyed by memory, it's almost laughable. Their faces, though, were no joke. The ironic thing was we all had shit, some dirtier than mine, just the weak link who couldn't keep it together. The unfortunate thing about this is not thoughts about how disappointed my parents would be or concerned. The humiliation felt was at the foot of strangers and committing an outrageous violation of my privacy. Amidst the joy, part of me cracked, reminding me of the reasons California was no longer home.

Ink, Sharpie, no Sharpie is much stronger, Expo. That is the scent filling my nose. My reflection is staring back at me, my face barely recognizable under the layers of dicks and illegible words. Hopefully, these few memories of yesterday will wash away as easily as the marks. My fingers ran through my hair, where the little sprouts of hair began to grow. Was it time to start again already? A choice lay before me: go back to the city, run away from this unwanted exposure.

Cigarette in hand, who was it who first drew blood and attracted the sharks? The room was empty. His face was walking away, the door closing behind him, tiles on my back, the off-white ceiling staring back at me. White lights pierced through my eyelids. Looking back, it was in a bathroom that triggered my memories—understanding the event that occurred that day. Where was the line drawn, and who stepped over it first? Couldn't shake the thought of it. Serena came down, lighting a cigarette in my company. "Do you recall much of what happened?" Here it comes. "Not much, I don't remember leaving the restaurant, but there are flashes of being in the shower with you holding me; sorry your clothes got wet." Her hand rested on my knee as if that could stop it from shaking. "You gave us all a good scare. You came back, sat on the couch, peed and started foaming at the mouth, Will and Luit carried you to the bathroom to throw up. They came and got me. We were alone when you were crying and muttering; *why couldn't he stop?* Put you in the shower to clean you up. You had alcohol poisoning, and as a minor here, if we had to call an ambulance, you get the idea," Has trauma become my identity? A living scar was just moving along. No, it hadn't crossed my mind in months, so why did it lie there after an indescribably good day? Fighting an idea, but it just came so naturally. She wiped away the last bit of dick sharpie that was left on my face, and within 24 hours, my ticket was booked home to my mom.

As with everything, there is a lesson in dotted lines, getting into the inner workings of my identity. It had been bottled up and finally burst. The release of it is a relief, and understanding the birth of an optimist is to realise a person must break into pieces to become an art. You have had your fill of life; anything that happens after is just dessert. My mom gave me two days to decide whether returning was best. It only took a day of being back in cold Vancouver to realise it was.

The Last Return

There was no sweet welcome back, but several new faces and one in particular that stood out: Stephanie.

We had work to do. There was always work to be done, whether it was in the mangrove nursery or watching our B.R.U.V drops and counting indicator species. All in an effort to be the emblematic reincarnation of the sharks we studied, contributing to something greater.

Stephanie Krots, if one could describe light to a blind man, it would be her laugh and warm presence. On a night when hearts were heavy, and it rained tequila sunrise, Stephanie told me about the times before the smiles and laughs. Her mother had died of cancer when she was nine, and the following year her father committed suicide only for her to be the one to find him; a few years after that, her brother died of a heroin overdose, and it was just her and her sister.

"The most advanced species that we know of and we still intentionally hurt others to make ourselves feel better."
(Stephanie Krots)

True intelligence is being able to see others and learn. She taught me about emotional equilibrium and watered the hedonistic seed that was sprouting inside me. To live amongst the pleasures of life. Its humidity clears a fog, power in the knowledge of the strength that we carry on our shoulders. Like that duck, it's okay if the rain falls; it will happen whether we wish it to or not. Requiring retribution after what had happened here, after what had happened so many times before.

Everyone was walking around in Santa hats on Christmas morning, and only about six volunteers remained over the holiday—those without family or those who had just had enough of them. The early morning was off at one of the villages to turn toilet paper rolls into shark cutouts with the kids. Painting them shades of blue and sticking fins on the sides. My sarong is covered in more paint than cloth. The drinking started after, and the staff let me forget that my drinking tolerance elapsed at one point by passing out beers. It was cute, Christmas music spin-offs played throughout the houses, and everyone had a secret Santa. My gift was an anatomically correct steel shark keychain given to me by a guy honoured to be called a friend. Just after sunset, we took a taxi into Suva to a pub called O'Reilly's. There are poles to dance on for the drunkenly inclined and several pool tables.

Shit, my purse was surrounded by a whole bunch

of other bags and jackets, and now, the other bags and jackets were gone, and my purse was still there, alone. Picking it up, the weight was the same, but you know when you've done something stupid and that your actions are about to show for it. My wallet had been stripped clean, cards gone, cash gone, and my cell phone in my pocket, which luckily always had an extra 20 bucks in the case. Something my dad always told me, "Never keep all your funds in one spot." Thanks, Dad.

"Stephanie, I've been pocketed, pickpocketed from my purse that wasn't in my pocket, regardless someone took all my shit, so can we go home now?" squishing my face, "Oh, one more game of pool and we go. I'll even buy you a drink; just enjoy." She was either good at pool, or her charms bewitched people into being bad. Walking out, we passed by just a tiny little alley that was only 50 feet long and about halfway down; this guy rushed past me and grabbed my purse, taking off with it. We were stunned by what just happened; looking at each other, we burst out laughing. Nothing was in it but a $15 purse and an empty five-dollar wallet. She hollered back at him, "Merry Christmas, ya filthy animal." I didn't know they got Home Alone in Australia. " That poor guy, he's going to go home thinking he just made some score and find absolutely nothing but a cheap bag."

Pride is a funny feeling, and it's like the welling up in your chest before you yell. We believe that if something really bad were to happen to someone we love, we are supposed to be capable of preventing it, and when we don't, we deny it was happening at all. We all dealt with our lack of normality in different ways. A month later, I left a place that taught me how to confront my trials and tribulations with a smile and a laugh because there will always be more.

Chapter Seven

Lemons

Why are lemons yellow, encased in the colour of happiness, sour to the taste and bitter to the rim.

Tim Hortons to the left of the convenience store to the right, the inside of the Vancouver airport was beginning to burn into my brain.

My return home was hardly a return at all, and it was beginning to feel like time was chasing me, slowly wrapping its hands around my neck and teasing me with thoughts of downfall, how sinful.

My taxi pulled into the apartment filled with moving boxes and suitcases. She was out of the house. Preparing to move, she said Europe would be better suited for people like us, unwanted in these parts of the world. Somewhere between my mother attending my brother's wedding and spending Christmas alone, she decided to go to Florence and set up a life. My suitcase is still packed with island necessities. The fridge is empty, and so is my stomach. Leaving it behind to walk to a place where meals were already prepared. Carderos was closed, and the wind misting off the water from the sea brought a chill. There's an old church just off the seawall. My mama brought us to church once or twice growing up, but we weren't religious folk; we talked about faith only in the comfort of our own house. With Cathartic intent, the bench in the back, about 15 rows from a preacher, sat a girl whose idea of the catholic church was that it was the biggest credit card of all. "God does not give us what we cannot handle" What does God know about the struggle, for he only watches. Just because you watch a movie about war doesn't mean you know what gunfire sounds like when it takes a life.

Most of the people in front just nodded in accordance with his words, over and over again, as if nodding was the payment for an entry to heaven. My ears turned to the women sitting just in front. They must have known because that cannot be a conversation one has so cavalierly in a church of all places. Talking about bleaching their dogs' butthole so that its colour was less obtrusive to the eye. Vancouver, where you either stand above everyone else or fall to their feet. There is evil in every part of this world because people extend to every part of it too. My skin was darker than it had ever been and now stained with ink. Church was nice, a reminder that even those with the most normal of lives can go crazy, but other than stale bread and cheap wine, they didn't have food.

27 April 2016

Sometimes lemons are sweet, strawberries are sour, and things don't always make sense, but there are two sides to every coin, and if you want to win every battle, you must see both sides for what they are. For a battle, be it big or small, requires one to fight.

Since the publication of the arrest came out, my email was linked to the Daily Journal to be notified when a post was made about his case.

Former fire chief to stand trial: Judge rules enough evidence for charges against Marc Ladas

"More than a year after the former fire chief of the Central County Fire Department was arrested for grand theft and tax evasion, a San Mateo County Superior Court judge agreed he should

answer to 10 felonies.

After two days of preliminary hearings culminated late Tuesday, a judge found prosecutors had enough evidence to proceed with a trial against Marc Ladas, according to District Attorney Bill Fisher.

In December 2014, Ladas pleaded not guilty to the 10 felony charges in a case prosecutors say was a "sophisticated" scheme between the former fire chief and his wife, Peta, who remains at large. The duo allegedly netted thousands of dollars by using fraudulent credit cards at a fake business controlled by the wife between January 2011 and June 2013."

The devil you know is better than the devil you don't. Anger diminished the man who contributed to my existence, and he became a lemon, regardless of memories of every daddy-daughter dance, trips to adventure lands and just quiet nights watching movies.

I've made amends with the fact they'll never win any Parent of the Year award, we can all agree, but they were and are good parents. They taught me to be strong and to love myself because sometimes that may be all you have. Fear is normal and beautiful; without fear, love is an empty letter full of hopeless words, and if you treat fear like a nuisance, you will surely suffocate in this life.

You can't kill fear, but it can die, and not many people experience its death if they do; they can typically remember the exact moment it happened. To put it in layman's terms, it might be that moment before someone decides they want to kill themselves, not a spur-of-the-moment suicide, one that is strategically planned and executed with thought. The alleviation of the responsibility of living because there was a moment you decided you were already dead. Gandhi experienced it, and it led to the well-known verse that *we accept the things we cannot change and change the things we cannot accept.* Gandhi succeeded in his reckless endeavours, for he accepted that he would die one day. That is inevitable, so why not play with it, thus making him one of the most successful activists in history. He achieved something rarer than striking oil in a rainforest. He made people care whether or not one man ate, not once but repeatedly. Hunger strike after hunger strike, as people pleaded for him to stop resisting our natural instinct: survival. If not taken as such an overwhelming profound display of sacrifice, you would compare it to an extremist child throwing a tantrum that played with the boundaries of life.

The mind seeks control bouncing back and forth from fixations to ludicrous conspiracies, it is not something you can tame, you can groom it, give it a clean cut, and allow society to try and sterilise it, but it will wander and fall and fly at the drop of a hat. When we fixate on the flexibility of conversation we fear not the unsaid word but the unconveyed thought that could have taken it further, for it may just spark a tantrum.

Receiving another message from him just the day before, warning me to protect myself that they were so close to finally catching her. It hurt me knowing he thought he was doing the right thing. If my dad was right, a knock at the door any day could have been to drag my mother off. His emails were probably just an attempt to will it into existence. There were flowers that grew outside my garden, and I wanted to see them. The devil you know is better than the devil you don't.

Our last and only month here passed slowly with dinners, drinks and carelessness until April when flights were booked.

Bahamas

A birthday is an odd thing to celebrate. Technically the only day that is your birthday is the day you're born, and every day after is an accumulation of days lived. So, on a day of this joyous accumulation of days when my mother asked what present would be suitable for her daughter, there was nothing greater than being back with my sharks. My sister, whose birthday was only five days after mine and her boyfriend joined me on this expedition. Perhaps a coercion from our mom to bond as siblings, the people we are today.

"You mother fucker!" Laci was tearing through my suitcase. "This is all mine." She exclaimed, holding up shirts and swimsuits. Introducing this new version of herself, who was confident and loud, "Why are you smiling?" couldn't help it, "Look at you strutting, getting angry, and what are you gonna do about it, have me walk around naked, this is all I packed." We set off on our first day on an excursion feeding iguanas with our mouths on sandy beaches off the main island of Nassau. "Just give them a kiss." Iguanas are vicious creatures, especially when you play with their food. The boat took us to a beach filled with pigs; sitting with them really lifts your body's confidence. My sister created a sweet moment with her boyfriend while my attention was occupied with trying to get one of the pigs to chase me to play tag, with our guide trying to hit on me. Guess there are more pigs in the water than expected, all to no avail. Taken after into the middle of the sea, provided with cheap snorkel gear; of course, my fancy dive mask came with me everywhere. The visibility was pristine, perfect for viewing the more than 20 reef sharks below. It was the first time being stripped of my equipment in the water with sharks; far more intimate the closer you get. Every movement is more direct and noticed, while everyone stays safely at the surface, watching their performances. That wasn't enough for me. Diving down as far as possible until my lungs felt crushed, and the guide swam after me. Trying to assure them, "No sir, I'm practically a professional." Just a bit of an over-exaggeration.

Worlds can collide and melt into each other—one of land and one of the sea. We didn't grow up with a community mentality, keeping each other typically at arm's length, but it's pretty easy to bond with someone travelling with a duffle bag full of cash. Seeing her grabbing onto the line starring, no, valuing something that was a reflection of a part of me no one from our world saw. Best birthday present. Still too nervous to let go of the rope, though, no matter how much taunting, teasing and tugging of the fins was applied.

We dove through forgotten sunken statues and even a shipwreck or two, embracing the changes that have developed over such a short period in the grand scheme of things. A certain metamorphosis was occurring before us, like intentionally driving on the wrong side of the road, waiting for headlights to appear, and asking if I was more likely to die merging into the lane paved for me or in the direction they told us not to go.

Chapter Eight

Counting Castles

Let the gates shut behind me into the empty castle; the furniture has been taken and the walls stripped bare. A mannequin with hands full of hair, for I am the lion with no courage, the tin man with no brain, the scarecrow with no heart, and Dorothy with no home, default through the fault of my own, just in a reality that lies in a phone, it holds me, bends me, and folds me strung up to dry, have you ever reached the point where you're begging to cry? The real breaking point isn't rock bottom; it's when you only feel something when you break a little more. So you begin to crave it because there are things in life far worse than being six feet under when you hold the shovel to dig your own grave, like an inescapable reputation.

<u>Amsterdam</u>
15 May 2016

The train into Amsterdam was lifeless, but the fields that it passed by were anything but. However, the book in my hands was nothing but a placeholder because my attention was drawn to the land. My Airbnb was right next to a french fry shop, so it always smelled like potatoes. Stephanie was in town; in fact, it was her last night—an odd coincidence, nothing more. My time here was intended to be alone until my sister arrived, but seeing her became a priority regardless of the reasons. Not to mention, it was Saint Patrick's Day.

It was the first time we had seen each other wearing so much clothing. We were laughing, eating, and reminiscing until it was drink after drink. She placed an edible arrangement of what was assumed to be MDMA in my mouth. It was the first time since California that anything synthetic had entered my bloodstream and invaded my mind. It tasted of butterfly wings, grits, and the start of other questionable decisions.

The lights beamed new colours that you could feel and smell; blue wasn't blue, but the sea and the green was freshly sprouted leaves, pink a budding flower between cement cracks and orange a zesty sun that felt like sorbet. "Drugs are bad for kids," she whispered as we danced further into the night.

Stephanie liked to show me new things. She took me to the famous Pink Elephant, where we were given dick-shaped lollipops and a pointy hat that said "Here For Now." They were famous for their live sex show, where they would display different genres of coitus intermittently. My favourite was the threesome; maybe they were just good performers, but it seemed to me they were enjoying it the most. Before the show ended, they asked for volunteers to come to the stage. Stephanie was Satan's wingman, as she volunteered me as a tribute to their erotic cause. Dick pops in hand, guided to the stage by a man with a wispy moustache. The willing and half-willing lined up to the side. Remaining at the back of the line, the last to be subjected to this. The star of the performance was a woman whose smile never cracked, though it did when she was alone, lying on her back, knees bent, holding a banana in the air. When a man (or woman) in a gorilla costume made it to centre stage, grabbing the banana and peeling it. Myself and the four other witnesses were stunned by what had happened next. The gorilla man placed the fully peeled banana into her vagina, with the majority of it sticking out. The man who led us to the stage then proceeded to announce. "Ladies and Gentlemen, please step forward and have a quick snack." The crowd roared with laughter as Stephanie ran to the front row to watch. My little sinner applauds my boldness. The gorilla banged on his chest, making gorilla noises as each person reduced the banana to a sliver. This was not hygienic at all. Next time, I suggest wearing goggles because, with closed eyes, executing such an act leaves room for error; you have to know precisely how far away your face can be. My long hair must have tickled her leg, because she flinched and nearly gave me my first lesbian experience. Worth it to see Stephanie laughing, mouth open, eyes pinched shut, and on the floor.

<u>Venice, Italy</u>
29 May 2016

The window sill is coated in a thin layer of settled air particles that are unable to be brushed away by the breeze. My fingers traced a smiley face; that's my thing now. Placing random smiling faces around the world so as to not forget to clean your shit. It's allergy season. Silly peasants probably thought it would keep the world smiling or cheesy. Nope, I identify as a conservationist after putting all those hours into cleaning up a world that keeps getting dirtier. The coffee shop below is full of men and women taking time to converse and enjoy the sun, but mostly drinking coffee and smoking cigarettes. The fumes of which filled my room; opening the window meant feeding my second-hand cravings, or maybe it just fed my need to indulge in the consistent lack of breath. Imagine living a wonderful life if you knowingly participate in an activity that shortens it—simply sadistic. Europeans are fancy, though, and much too fancy to participate in something as lowly as smoking an industrial cigarette; no, that would be barbaric. Here, cigarettes are hand-rolled, each one a tiny work of carcinogenic art. We spent most days wandering around museums and narrow streets, getting lost in being lost. Taking trains to town we couldn't pronounce.

My mother had finally joined us in Italy, and to celebrate all of us being together again, Laci suggested we go to Venice to try a Bellini from a bar that, in the 1930s, wrote its own history. Our apartment hung in the centre of Florence, across from the leather market, where hides and furs were tossed about. To anyone struggling with self-esteem, it would be wise to walk through because no less than 30 Italian men will tell you just how beautiful you look, but what is beauty if not complemented by a blue mink coat? Of course, my mother had already bought three, which now sat staring at me from her bed. She was here next to me, both of us glued to our laptops.

"There, booked!"

"Did you know Italy is going to drown one day?"

"Then it's a good thing we're gonna see it now; look, this is where we're staying." A palace overlooking the canals, a rather large upgrade to the big redbeacon we slept in once a long time ago.

My sister's anxiety used to exhaust her, like screaming underwater; it was useless, and if done for long enough, it would drown her, and she would retreat into herself. Now she commands; an award for most improved goes to my darling sister. The award for highest body count goes to m— actually, it still goes to my brother.

The reservation was booked for 4:00 p.m., at Harry's Bar, located across from the Giardini Reali. My mother had already opened a bottle of prosecco, pouring three glasses full. My sister rolled her eyes at our lack of time management. Succumbing to our vanity overruled anyone's dictation of our time. Laci disagreed with our lack of consideration. She left quite angrily, I might add. Running down the streets of Venice, whereas those who remained took a water taxi. The gondolas are quant, and the water, even if there was a shark in it, couldn't get me in. Life is multi-dimensional once you strip the barricades and throw yourself where the money lands.

My mother showed up with her boyfriend, Giovanni, on her arm. He was tall enough to be her man and obedient enough to know when to speak; so far, he was my favourite. His job, though, remained a mystery; whatever he did kept him comfortable. His eyes darted from one end of the table to the other, ravaging through rounds of bellinis and, of course, as a true fan of Ernest Hemingway, a Manhattan. After ordering most of the menu and attempting to clear out the liquor cabinet, the owner came out and said, "Thank you. Hope you are enjoying everything? Did you try the ravioli?" My mother scoffed as if she knew more than the chef boyardee tin cans we grew up with. *"Ravioli, really?"* And he said, *"You trust me; you trust an Italian when he says to try the ravioli. On the house."* Giovani was silent, which was odd for him; he always complimented my mother nicely in both appearance and companionship. She smiled more, and it wasn't for any reason other than a complete lack of control to prevent it. She was free. I pulled my napkin aside as the table was left prepped for the next course, which was apparently ravioli. My hand found my mom's, and she squeezed. *"Happy?"* A look stained with mea culpa. *"How could I not be, Mom."* The ravioli was thin as a piece of paper and as good as he recommended. Our compliments must have gone far because he stayed at our table the rest of the night, telling stories about the bar. "On 13th May 1931, Giuseppe Cipriani Senior opened this bar. It is the place for writers, painters, artists, kings, queens, and aristocrats to congregate and mould this city." My mother had a way of charming people; maybe it was her uniqueness, for who finds a rare flower and relinquishes it so easily.

Santorini, Greece
7 April 2016

"Kill, fuck, or marry Poseidon, Zeus, or Hades."

"Easy, kill Hades, fuck Poseidon, marry Zeus."

"No, incorrect. Kill Zeus, fuck Hades, marry Poseidon, and with the death of Zeus, rule over the sky and sea with him as empress of the world."

"That wouldn't work if you fucked Hades. Poseidon

would not marry you, and all the sons of Zeus's children would overthrow you because you killed their father; I'd kill Hades just for his dog."

"Shut up and finish your milkshake, Laci."

A conversation bespoken at the foot of the Greek Theatre at the Acropolis, and maybe these gods would hear us, finally smiting us for our foul behaviour. Well, at least mine. Travelling with her was like a never-ending museum. Every hotel was five-star, every flight was business class, and every second was an opportunity to learn. We were grabbing life by its historical balls.

This morning we went swimming in the Petalioi Gulf and, the following day, had a ferry to Santorini, then Sparta to see the olive farms. We travelled like a rock skipping over still water. It made me wonder; no one ever came out crying, except maybe my dad. She never had to lick anyone's wounds that she created with her "sophisticated schemes," as the daily journal called it. It wasn't her against a poverty-stricken family. It was her against the government, her against the state and borders, and her against my father. Is a victimless crime really a crime, or is someone just mad that someone thought of something before anyone else, and a female person of colour at that? Fascinating.

Greece was connected to my father's roots and, therefore, mine. It's where his grandfather was born and came over to Ellis Island, where the first Ladas landed. Now, it's the place that holds my freedom from attachment and the knowledge that no matter what shall pass before my eyes, my own culpability to rise above it shall remain unhindered, in a way like a sea. Its pollution levels may increase, causing acidification, but its ability to rejuvenate a sustainable ecosystem does not falter. Who am I to scold the wind for being too strong? To see it as a nuisance that sweeps my hair when its power has the ability to sail ships and spread seeds.

I'm glad we didn't check the bed that day, for if not, these white sheets that encompass me now might be wrapping my body far underground in a world unseen. If not by my hand, then the pills or drinking. Now, if not a plane, walking, buses, or a canoe would do. Escapism is an art, after all. "Where will you go next?" "Not sure, maybe France; do some solo camping." Looking worried, she said, "Sounds like a bad idea to go alone, and we are black—we don't camp."

"And if it's a mistake, I will find out sooner or later, but for now, I choose to take a chance."

"Why must you be so dramatic?"

"Because if a shark stops swimming, it will die."

"That doesn't even make sense."

France
Almost June

When you're travelling alone, trust is like having a drunk friend supervise on a night out. La Route des Cretes La Ciotat extended around the cliff side of Cassis. A stranger by name but friend by heart took me to the top of the peak, where you could see a little area to make work for camp. The sun was due to set in about an hour.

My timing wasn't the best; about halfway up, the sunset and my headphones prevented the quiet from invading. The idea of being alone in dark silence, walking in an upward direction with no service, no knowledge of the area, just one foot over the other, is mentally unsettling.

My bag was crammed with the soup that would taste good cold, two bananas squashed under the weight of my three apples, two big bags of nuts, rolling tobacco, extra filters, raw papers, all the essentials, and about 16L of water. I figured that would be enough, given that my body is used to operating on borderline dehydration. I'm not the biggest fan of how water tastes. The only tent available was for four people. The big, blue obnoxious housing unit had to be carried by hand like a cumbersome child, and it got in the way a lot. Every step brushes my leg, leaving a slight white scratch from the metal clasp.

Along the edge, the sea made sounds but hid in the abyssal shadows.

After a restless sleep and waking to sherbet skies, the word dawn just felt so right for this setting, gentle, not fragile, but soft.

If it weren't bad for the environment, this shitty tent would have stayed right where it was. Packing it back into the bag from which it came was hazardous, especially when considering my tendencies to be the aggressive type. After an hour of hiking down with a fully opened tent in hand, it managed to squeeze back in at about the point of taking an afternoon break. There was a man-made clearing, but no men were present, finding it was a happy accident. Regardless of who may enter, my clothes are stripped off and I am eternally barefoot.

I close my book of choice as the last page of Elegance of a Hedgehog by Muriel Barabery comes to an end; it felt only right to read a book by a French author when roaming around French lands. Hello, rock friend, crab, shell, and leaf. There is a belief that something does not hold consciousness until it is named, forging an identity as separate entities. Odd measures were put in place to function within certain parameters of society. Do the ants name the trees and bees, or is it just a reaction to their existence? Food, predator, and prey. Perhaps Dr Seuss had similar thoughts when writing about thing one and thing two. I've gotten asked over the years how I've held onto my sanity, and the truth is, I don't think I had it to begin with.

Maybe do some push-ups—one, two, fuck that. No, who am I? A frat boy, perhaps meditating. Meditating might not be for us ADHD folk. In part, the fly is to blame for it not leaving my side. All of the squirming covered my hands in the dust. White dust, like the residue the pills left, surrounded by a background that was anywhere but there. I haven't heard my voice in 24 hours, except for the occasional swear words.

"Hi there, lady; I am the woman in the mirror." Trying to picture myself sitting across from me would have been easier if I was high, but I managed to make a pretty good blurry, broken-down girl.

"Until now, you have been forgotten—not everything you went through, just that moment. We didn't tell anyone either. No pity points for us. You are still hurt sometimes, but it's better. You know, there probably is a parallel universe where our attempt was successful. Dad would be the one to find us. That would have been cruel. We still have a lot to figure out, but we have done and seen some pretty cool shit. We still pull out our hair, but I'm proud of us. Mom is happy, and in love. We've never been in love, and I don't know if we'll be very good at it. Giving ourselves and all our baggage to someone. Laci is good at it or she hides well. We are not meant for such mergers; their decisions alter our own. Pretty cool to try it out like a sweater in a store, preferably not French. I get why they don't like it when people try to speak French because when they speak English, they make me wish a tomato-sized cork existed to shove in their mouths. I wish I could hug you, but you hugged yourself that day; there is strength in that. Well I am you so by that logic, I hugged you; love a good paradox." In my projected mind, she got up and walked away peacefully even with my stifled attempts at confronting my feelings. As for now, maybe I should just rest, close my eyes, and be present.

The forest is submerged in this pastel hue; the green is almost green, but it's not quite sure, as if fading into indecisiveness. This is my gym, where I remain physically fit and conscientiously unaware that every step taken feeds my six-pack because my music is louder than my muscle pain. Thank you, My Sentimental Friend, by Herman's Hermits, that has been on loop in my ears for over an hour now.

The initial rush of reality faded into a structured society. The first people in sight were a couple, young, laughing and looking back at each other every few seconds just to make sure they were still there smiling at the confirmation. Me and my two bees, a buzz—what's all the fuzz about?

Right under the cliffside on a hidden beach were small clearings carved out amongst the palms. I stripped my body bare again, setting up my backpack as a pillow; the ground was my mattress, and my blanket was just my blanket. If there is one luxury not to give up in solitude, it is the comfort of residing under a fabric sheet.

Hair matted skin darkened from layers of dirt and my odour, dirtier. Cleansed by the submergence into the ocean.

A floating tin can shimmering in the sky above me, a man on a rock reeling a line and two lovers jointly entwined. Have you ever seen a man fishing from the window of a plane 10,000 feet in the air? Me neither, but imagine how far you would have to zoom in even to picture the outline of his rod. So significantly insignificant. Important in our version of now, but within the understanding that there are billions of "nows" going on right now and every now after.

In this fisherman's now, his dog is chasing the winds, and he is waving to a woman in the sea whose head barely peaks above the water, trying to discreetly wash away the dirt from all regions of her body. Maybe there was a tug on his line, or he simply wanted a conversation.

His hair was short and well-kept; a clean-cut fisherman was something you would only find in a town near Marseille. His sleeping bag was crushed next to a few cans of empty beer. High on his rock, looking down on me, wrapped in a damp sandy blanket. Putting on my best accent, I said, "Bonjour monsieur."

An accent not good enough to fool anyone let alone an actual Frenchman, " Bonjour, pouvez-vous surveiller mes affaires pendant que je vais à ma voiture." Wow, that was a lot of words I didn't know. "I'm sorry, I don't speak french," I said in English though, as if French was my first language. He pointed to me, then my eyes, then his things. "You want me to watch your things! Of course." I nodded in agreement, hoping universal sign language would do. It must have been because he stretched down and disappeared with his dog into the trees.

Burying my toes in the sand as the watchful guard man. The sun had said goodbye to the day as he returned with beers in hand. Handing me one "Merci." Though our exchange ended, I wasn't compelled to leave, nor was he inclined to make me. Constructing ourselves as the space around us once did, we sat and drank to the sounds of the water, wind, and nothing more until my eyes grew weary enough to crawl into my nature-made shelter and stare into the stars staring back at me, I prefer an endless ceiling.

In this brief second, my hands are in my hair, and the only person who can stop me is me. Enough willpower to drag my ass to the top of this mountain, a mere foot from the edge of a cliff, set up a place to sleep, wake up at 5 a.m., shower with the sunrise, follow the steps back, and yet the will to stop pulling out my hair is unfathomable. There is no hair salon here, no currency in solitude; the trees don't take credit cards. Perhaps I am slowly starting to lose the last scraps of my sanity. I have spent a lot of time talking to trees lately.

Chapter Nine

Las cosas inmortales

7 June 2016

"*Don't die in Mexico, you don't have life insurance.*" It was the last message she sent me after my arrival here. She hid me away at my request for witness protection, my father wanted me to go back, go on trail for things he did not do, but whose truth was I speak to, for my own would certainly hold no weight. Proper sleep has evaded me for months since the messages from my father became rampant, even if left unanswered. There's a recurring dream where I'm in an old Victorian house and on my knees. There are two guns being pointed at either side of my head, two barrels pressed up against my temples, and a silver coin resting in my hand; it shines when you rock it back and forth. On one side is my father's name, and on the other is my mother's. Flicking it into the air, rotating its sides, but someone pulls the trigger before it lands. I am beginning to envy those in a coma. Is that a mental extension or just an illogical fallacy arguing moral constructs?

Manzanillo, home to a crocodile and sea turtle reserve, just outside any inhabiting towns, on a hammock woven by synthetic wraps. The waves pounding just outside earshot. There's no hot water, and the shower has a single stream that pokes out of a cement wall and the mosquitoes are well fed.

As rock that sinks to the sea floor, makes a temporary sand bed until the current moves again, I continue to do the same.

Prehistoric beings are deities—ancestors with secrets of unshared knowledge communicating through dominance and raw, calculated behaviour. Their instinctiveness is tied to something I'm only starting to see.

Hercules; my favourite long tailed deep eyed dinosaur. Rescued when he was only eight months old, with most of his body caught tangled in wire, leaving him scarred, raging like a blender, and having an unsatisfiable temper.

A strong name is befitting our world's functioning fossils; Hercules is a story about a boy burdened at birth to struggle with overcoming 12 humiliating, arduous tasks cast down by a scorned woman, Hera.

Confronting each of his enemies, one after the other, slaying them all, eventually conquering Cerberus, a big fluffy dog that guarded the gates of Hell.

Would Hercules have been able to slay his demons and be welcomed by the gods if not for his meticulous training? Would any person born of simplicity be able to conquer such a feat if they were just dropped in precariously? No, my father, a prime example, was dropped into my mother's world like this, and it ate him whole. Leaving him wounded, supposing that my mother was Hera and the judicial system of California was his Cerberus.

Some grow up and discover what their parents are capable of, I've always known. It looks like the sinking eyes of a crocodile, and home shouldn't lie in the eyes of a crocodile.

Black Sand Beach Bar

There's a woman here; Rosalie. Sweet, older than me, and yet far more naive. She's from a small town in India, where her parents provide servants who clean the house, prepare meals, and help her with her studies. *Comfortable* money, she learned how to sweep for the first time this morning. She has never been away from home and showed me a rare side of purity that only a few get to experience. She has never drank, kissed a man, or held the hand of a stranger. Yet here she stands thousands of miles away from home, free to make decisions just like that. A moment is powerful as long as you decide to seize it. Jiacomo must have thought the same thing.

"No, no ladies; when there is a man present, he sweeps." His words were always more smug when he wore black.

"Well, when a man presents himself, I will hand him the broom."

"I can show you a man."

"Go away, Jiacomo; you are not invited to participate in this class." You've got to love Italians; they've got meatballs of steel.

Around four o'clock, she bestowed on me, a 17-year-old, the honour of buying her first shot. She's 24. She reminds me of my sister in both composure and appearance. Those who face anxiety typically have strict discipline to keep themselves in order, regulating their good and bad mannerisms. If discipline combats anxiety, then a disciple of unstructured disinhibition is freed by complete lack of awareness.

The winds were picking up at the beach bar. It was not the decision to start drinking so early that was the problem; it was the fact that the idea was to come to the beach to go surfing.

Out past the breaking point by finding the calm pass. The sun toasted me in the still before the build, and the lifeguard would have had an easy day if it had ended there. However, if ifs and buts were candies and nuts, we would all have a merry Christmas.

Everything happens in an instant. Your body reacts before your mind has a chance to process it. A distorted mind does not leave you with good odds of success. The size of the wave became apparent as it was the last thing to fill my vision.

There was no fight, and that's what saved me. My body relaxed, guided by the rush of the pull. Seconds felt like minutes, with the leash dragging me forward and twisting around my ankle. Still a stretch out, and no bodies in the water, dragged to the side of the rocks that hid me from the bar. Until that one final wave threw me into an oversized pebble that protruded out, bent a little to the left, snagging the corner of my jaw, my ribs ramming into the rocks that pinned me against the water, truly between a rock and a hard place.

"*Hoy no es tu dia, suerte que te vimos antes que un cocodrilo* (today is not your day; lucky we saw you before a crocodile did)".

There's not much to say with the washing waves where you crash, you leave your mark and simultaneously a mark is left on you.

One Way Home

Cahuita, a rescue centre for turtles, leatherbacks, and green seas in sunken, rough blue tanks—babies carried by the bucket transported to safer grounds. Around eleven at night to two in the morning, we would ride ATVs or take walks along the beach, spotting turtles nesting. Then, provided we found some, which we always did, we would take the eggs to the centre where they could incubate safely. Hatchlings would have torn up their fins from nibbling at each other because, believe it or not, baby turtles can be dicks, and all of this is to prevent poachers from capturing and selling them to local markets for soup.

To be a tourist who barely speaks the language coming into a land that is not mine and telling those who have been here for generations how to live. What they should and shouldn't do by going out of our way to stop them from making a living. Pretty horrendous when you put it that way. To give to something requires you to take from another. Balance can seem unachievable, but if you stand for nothing, then you might as well sit down. However, an animal has no right to be compared to a dollar, but neither does a father feeding his children. These are not monetary things yet hold monetary value. Even here, money commands and demands the most, calling into question ethical boundaries.

In my pursuit of discovering, as my mother would say, my mental extensions, I have discovered that America lives uncomfortably, deemed at the forefront of progression (in the eyes of Americans and anyone else who idealises the American dream) because when a society is uncomfortable, they focus on the adaptations that can be made for the sake of convenience because they equate comfort with access. In actuality, with the cultures encountered thus far, comfort is just comfortable. It's undisturbed by ideas of inadequacy. A simple cup of coffee or cigarette can act as an anti-inflammatory for a swollen mind.

Though my mother is Jamaican, Bob Marley's

belief that wealth doesn't come from a bank does not register with her. The home consisted of shiny toys that distracted all of us from asking questions. Our silence was her convenience, demonstrating that we were doing okay financially, and the price tag measured the means. Parents can buy toys to show love; it doesn't make them bad parents or bad people for lacking a more valid form of expression. It just makes the exchange hollow and will eventually trickle down into an unhealthy relationship with possession. Though it's easy to say I'm not attached to things because of how often I've left everything behind, in a way, it's kind of easy once you've seen your mother throw a 2,000-dollar laptop off a cliff, twice.

"*Stop biting the toothbrush, you little shit.*" I was tempted to bite his flipper for fighting me. "Teaha, don't swear at the turtles." Rosalie had the calmest in her hands, unable to relate to my current struggles. "He keeps biting the bristles on the toothbrush; how is she gonna survive in the sea if she enjoys eating plastic? Her name is now Turdle," accentuating the first syllable in her newly bestowed name. "Put him in the bucket;

it's time to release them."

"I'll hold Turd; we've bonded," holding him up to my face, like a family photo.

"For fucks sake, just come on." Rosalie, from poised to impatient.

"Now, who's swearing in front of the turtles, Rose?" She's grown so much these past few weeks. Even yesterday, she ran naked drunk into the sea, declaring, "We're gonna save every last one of you." It was beautifully optimistic. Freedom comes in stages—in solitude and in the comfort of friends you trust. She could have broken down last night into the worst version of herself. Being a safe space for someone is freedom for both you and them.

The bucket poured out 109 little leather backs, clean shells ready for their grand seascape. "Turd, we've only known each other for about 30 minutes, but that's your whole life so far. Please don't die; reproduce lots of babies and stay away from plastic." My lips pressed against his little bobblehead, and she joined her sisters.

In their wordless ways, the turtles taught me that if you stay on the beach where predators are abundant, you only have time to be prey. Spending too much time talking about who you are or who you want to be, you will never actually have enough time to embody that vision and instead fall to the will of the masses. That is why they scurry from egg to shell to sea. If only they had a dollar to spend, would their direction change?

Last Night

Travellers make me laugh, some may order food from a Thai restaurant; others may go to Thailand and just call it food in search of authenticity. It's difficult to escape the image others have created for you. Travellers are soft, temporarily freed from past judgements and a pigeonholed past. We sit on rocks by the beach watching sunsets, thinking how could anyone not want this lifestyle. They are the lovemakers, philosophers, and tangents in the rat race. To be loved by a traveller is to always be second to the world, like falling in love with a painting and someone telling you to ignore the picture and look at the brush used to paint it. People are as necessary as brushes, which is very true; you cannot paint without them, but they are second to none as the more that is created on the canvas.

I am no expert in love, simply an observer. Seventeen years in this world, sexually active for three of them, and today was the first time my day started with a man in my bed who wasn't in my way.

We experience many realities of love over the precipice of time, the most shameful being that sometimes we care more to be loved than to love another, and the saddest part is that until we find the person who creates our last definition of love, we spend our time only capable of partly loving everyone else.

You can't fall in love until you suffer. Though it seems people mistake a broken heart for unfulfilled expectations. It is not a battle to be won or lost. It's a race in which the end is never in sight. You just keep running. It is immeasurable—an illness with no cure. It is a joyous triumph to see who sits there waiting to congratulate you for making it this far without them. It is in our nature, when we are lost or overwhelmed, to wonder in lust and depravity; capitalise on our own misdeeds. Infatuation, obsession is a weak love; if bottled, you could drink a case of it and not get drunk.

Even if you can come to an understanding of why we're still left with how it is an annoyance compared to the chewing gum on my jeans. So to the person who sits at the top waiting for me, please be patient because the journey towards you requires falling a lot when one knows nothing of romantic love and everything of heartbreak, but with every step, it's a bit closer. When I do fall, let it be like floating feathers caressed by the land in the arms of another, for many say when you die, you die alone, but you are dead, and you have no perception of loneliness. In fact, it is the only occasion on which we truly know nothing.

Costa Rica
27 August 2016

My legs are tired and mind more so, these past few weeks, I've been alone. No one's thoughts are in my mind but my own. The air in the plane is starting to clog my lungs; and it's getting hard to breathe as my embodied persona of the unsettled nomadic wanderer continues to cascade around the world running from and towards occupied pockets of space.

Hundred thousand colon was my current net worth abroad, which might have seemed like a lot of money, but honestly, it was only about $150. Half of which had to be used on the hour-long taxi ride to the boarding school that my mother thought would be best to give me some direction. Normal has begun to be equated with inadequate. An uneasy and long-forgotten expectation of being in place until graduation began to grow.

The driver gave me a cheeky smile and returned my luggage. It was so fucking humid that my hair lifting off my shoulders into a little nest was audible.

10 September 2016

She handed me a form and said, "Yes, you will need an adult to sign you out for the weekend if you plan to be out overnight." After years of being my guardian, needing supervision for a single night was an outrageous thought. Age is becoming more of a limitation than ever in a place meant to encourage and build my freedoms. Even just having a sleepover with a friend required documentation. Grabbing the documentation, I asked, "Can my mom call and excuse the need for this because a babysitter is pretty unnecessary at this point." didn't change the outcome.

Tamarindo is known for many things; ski shots, coke and surfing. The bar Loose Moose located between some sand and the sea washed beach had an endless supply.

It was 5 a.m., and my body was burnt out from an

exhausting day. There was a boy, surfer with dark skin and eyes to swim in, whose bed was as tempting and close by as another ski shot.

For some reason, my hangovers always seem to consist of waking up super early, my quiet escape began around 8 o'clock, with his arm stretched over me. To say the night with him was less than satisfactory would be an understatement. I went down the stairs to wake up my friend, who was snoring on his couch with a pool of drool under her chin. "Maddie, Maddie, we gotta go, we gotta go." Her wide-eyed confusion shot her out of the imprinted couch. Hand in hand, cracking open the main door, I heard from upstairs a slight call, "Teaha?" In an uproar of giggles, we sprinted out of his house. You could say the night had LITTLE expectations, and even those fell SHORT. A SMALL inconvenience, a SHRIMP cocktail. Pobrecito.

Living as if the days were still temporary, snorting each day away. When something lacks permanence, you don't understand why people give a shit. The students are treated like children, so that's what we remained. If patience is a blowjob, people are starting to hit the back of my throat.

It's these same situations over and over again,

finding myself locked in a haze. Regardless of any form my attendance back on school grounds was expected as of Sunday night by 7pm, I was back by 5. Walking where the trimmed lawn meets the growing weeds and standing trees. Howler monkeys screaming songs to pierce to silence. Even amongst the wild things it is still not quite right. More of myself continues to become unrecognisable, it is the times when I am around others I feel the loneliest and in solitude companionship.

After a few fuzzy months, there was a nagging little itch that was not enough.

"Mom, they're children; I can't do this without you."

"What are you talking about? We called just last week, and you were cliff jumping and rappelling down waterfalls." Good point. "Yes, but none of it was done sober, and I am Goldilocks now, and this bed is too small." And simply unmade, she lingered on the line, "We're moving to Spain next week; you really liked France, right? Like the same thing, do you want to come?"

"Fuck yes, book my ticket." Life was odd now that my mother had replaced her shackles with a diamond tennis bracelet.

Chapter Ten

Momentos de Impactos

Spain

She wrapped her arms around me, burying her face in my white button-up. *"Embrace the heartbreak, for it is a reminder that you have one."*

Something both of my parents sorely lack is peace. My mother's inability to seek out simplicity has left her in a state of content maliciousness, contesting the actions of others.

Heartbreak; there's no real definition for it; just something vital that no longer functions. We use the word cavalierly, though; heartbroken implies it can't be fixed, and saying heart damaged doesn't sound as poetic.

My mother held a work conference at the house, associates, all men. They were her power cell, draining her just as much as they gave her energy. More and more about her world makes sense, and a growing seed inside me feels drawn to it. Quien con fuego juega se quema.

She said to me after, seeing my growing interest, "Spend time with yourself and you will see exactly what you are capable of. You are attached to nothing and fear only shallow losses at this age. Even death is something that will un-phase you because you are without roots and whatever roots you had, you ripped out. The world will look at what you have accomplished and say you are lucky and therefore you will never understand the days you cry yourself to sleep." She told me about her work that night and how it operated. How I am following in her footsteps just in much nicer shoes and that there will be a day when I restart and in the shadows of the world I will stop lying to myself.

Children can't help but become a version of the people that nurtured their existence. I might say my younger years were forgotten, but where do they lie if not my memory.

Surrealists

A new girl in December is like going to the same museum every day and seeing the same paintings, which makes the arrival of a new one rather exciting.

Charles Darwin. Assimilate with no one, and you will align with everyone. To control your setting, you must adapt. When you get treated like an option, remind them how many you have. As the new girl, you have many; the men know this too. The new girl is sought after, and no one fights over a position no one else wants. Walk down a hallway; all eyes are on you, observing. People are simple as long as you don't give them time to become more than just that—a slight alleviation of the burden of loneliness.

People act in accordance with social laws. Abject tools and steps in the ladder to attend the most gratifying and memorable events. Manipulation, if you will, is not as shallow as it sounds. Everyone uses everyone, for you are useless if you cannot be used. Remember not to misuse or abuse, and the relationship will remain mutually beneficial. There are three great fears associated with this.

1. Fear of missing out: The moment
2. Fear of finding out: Yourself
3. Fear for what may come: The future

There's a certain group in every school, I call them the implementers, they walk around like a NIKE just do it advertisement. Month after month, it's becoming more apparent that opening up to people is a struggle for me. When you spend enough time with someone, they actually want to know things about you, and these are the people who could remove the magnifying glass pressed against my persona. If an eye for an eye makes the whole world blind, what is it when you give someone insight? For as much as I have learned about human behaviour, how much of my personality is a facade. Oddly enough, I wish my father was here, people are more difficult to understand than sharks.

Inspiring people create inspiring settings: Basquiat, Warhol, René Magritte, and Dali. Visionariaries with obscure visions, and when words fail, art prevails. You don't know what has the potential to inspire you until you've done something greater than what you've already experienced. Passion combats procrastination, and what is passion if not the inspiration drawn from an idea you've yet to have?

"Pull over!"

"Why? They're out of season." The audacity of this man to think that the grape's ripeness would really prevent me from eating it. "Sir, I have never eaten grapes straight from a vineyard in Spain. If you don't stop this car, I will open the door and jump out."

Making a wise decision, the car stopped in front of this canal dugout made of sand and just behind rows upon rows of bushels of grapes. Some were dark and others pale in comparison, and handful by handful, we all ate. Unripened grapes flew as the boys threw a perfectly good snack at each other. We weren't high on anything, but each other's company.

We drove until the car pulled in a dirt lot approaching two paths. The four boys walked ahead as my feet couldn't help but drag at the sight of the intended cliff we were supposed to jump off of. The lake was green and the depth of the water was unknown. Like the swamps the crocodiles would hide. One by one, they lept, jumping repeatedly doing backflips like they had been training their whole lives, except for one of the guys who sat with me because there's no way in hell he was jumping either. My toes lingered over the edge, my whole body paralyzed at the height, one slip, one movement and I would fall with no one to catch me.

We've been here for six months now and still there was a constant reminder that maybe we shouldn't. The air got thicker, and my chest would tighten at the mention of his name or untimely emails, the same feeling as standing on the edge of that cliff, never did he mention my happiness, just cause for concern. He stopped asking me where I was and started telling me where I had been, a not-so-friendly reminder that the FBI also has Instagram. A fugitive by association is still a fugitive. Yet, as this place became a marker I still wish he was here.

Needle in Stacks
6 May 2017

Former fire chief gets three years of probation and three months in jail, while his wife remains at large. The daily journal really should spice up its headlines and make them more dramatic.

My dad pleaded guilty, ending his case favourably for the judicial system he supports. Existing in the lines of irony, where obsession and an inability to disattach coexist. He stayed in California to fight for his legacy and its people, more attached to them than he ever was to me.

One fist, two fist, red fist, blue fist. Anger in the form of blood coming off my knuckles and dents in a wall. Our fishbowl shrank to just the top floor, empty and mine, with a room just on the left for unused dishes and pots. The occupants of the rest of the house ceased to exist. It was just me, my anger, and some pots that would look better in pieces. There are rooms now where you can go and break shit, but it's a far drive, and this is just down the hall. A clay pot about the size of a salad bowl had a one-on-one fight with the floor; it lost. Then glass after plate until every fragile thing in sight combusted, crumbling onto the tile floor, a wasteland, one for every wasted tear. A soured seed planted in barren lands bearing poisonous fruit and I am the gardener.

There's a copy of *Who Moved The Cheese* in a small dresser beside my mother's bed. When you travel as much as we do, there are always a handful of things that always get packed. His favourite book, with the blue cover and red binding. It's hard to forget the past when trauma bonds you to it. My mom doesn't have many other kinds of bonds. She loved him even when he threatened her security and then mine.

It had been almost four years since his arrest, and no knock at the door had ever come. Being afraid became as useful as a heater in the desert. With every obstacle faced thus far, fear shouldn't be scary, just acknowledged and understood. My twisted sinner was born of fear, chaos, and rage, wanting nothing but to overpower others to control what was once deemed uncontrollable.

Anger is productive, sitting amongst the carnage. The mess was cleaned up, and the day moved on. The only unfortunate thing to come from it was that my mother heard.

"*Baby*, you okay?" Her maternal nature knew when it was needed. "Yeah, I just needed to smash a few bottles." Nodding in understanding, she said, "Okay, pack a bag, we're going to London on Friday, and maybe try writing something." Not a bad idea.

Hi Dad,

How do I look you in the eyes if I ever get the chance? You stole my good night's sleep like a mosquito in my ear for years and years. Until I hid under the covers and never came out. I drink whiskey because you hated it. I look like her, and you hated it. I grew up, and you hated it. The truth is that the idea of me will always be better than the reality. You'll never say abandoned because the picture you painted is stained in the colour of my faults washed into the grey murk, dipped and forgotten. I hope you find peace, for it is more pleasant than the pain you shoulder, and when this passes, let us start over because I only have one of you, and though that may be undeserving, on whose side is unknown. There is hope for the father who danced, laughed, and cried with me; there is still so much of you that I see in me, and one day you will choose me, or I will no longer be a choice. I wish you luck, and if you can't buy your way out of serving time, don't drop the soap.

We stood in line at the airport Sunday evening, waiting to pass through immigration. We knew our visas were expired, but that's never really been an issue. With Spaniards, if it doesn't come with a glass of wine, it doesn't need attention, but today the officer was extra meticulous, and when he saw that our stamp was well past its due date, he informed me, "You can't enter into Spain or Europe." This poses a problem because my biology exam is coming up. My mom passed without issue and resided on the other side, waiting for me. I gestured to her to go, handling it by myself from this side. "Excuse me, Miss, you're gonna have to go to the office over there to the left and speak to one of the officers who will handle your deportation." My mother came back into the mess that was about to go down. "That's my daughter." Yet before we could even say a word, we were being escorted to a room with only two empty chairs and a man whose English was as poor as my mother's Spanish. It came across clearly enough that we had the option to be deported back to Canada or figure out something else, we had thirty minutes. My mom had booked us two tickets back to London, and we were on the next flight out.

To be fair, handling it alone would have just been me calling her from the other side and booking one ticket instead of two, but it brought me back to that day when I would have refused to leave her side and now here I am with her.

Pretending to fix a clasp on my bag, I whispered to the concierge, "Please send up two bottles of red wine and anything chocolate." There are times when you just have to know what someone needs without them asking for it.

Drunken words began to flow, "Our family is pretty

fucking far from normal. Don't get me wrong; nothing in this world could ever make me ask for a different one, but damn. We were like the lower-budget, crime-fueled Kardashians. We got deported together, and the funniest part is that it wasn't our first time getting deported. " Grinning with wine-coloured cheeks, she said, "Of course, you're a child, Tea, and sometimes you forget that. When I'm not there, you're stronger and smarter for it. My job is to dictate necessity; at this rate, you will become me faster than I did."

We spent two weeks in a four-star hotel getting our hair, nails, and eyelashes done and shopping at Victoria's Secret. Manicured and looking fine for no one but us, we had dinners and lunches at the hotel while my studies took place, and she conceded a whole escape back into Spain by flying to Gibraltar, which was owned by the UK, where we spent three nights on a yacht hotel, hiked up to the top of the Gibraltar rock to see all the monkeys, and then just walked across the border where nobody checked the stamps. Then on the train back to Barcelona just in time for my biology exam.

Life with her was always shiny: Sundays at fancy hotel bars, playing pool, driving to school in an Alfa

Romeo, and then in a Mercedes SUV the next month. One afternoon in the parking lot, the spot the car was parked in was just a bit too tight, denting the entire passenger door. There was no scolding or angry aftermath, just a replacement in the garage the next day.

A night when my words were riddled with foul language with her. Her need for power trickled into our relationship with her violent reminder that I was independent as long as she allowed me to be. The fight resulted in me stripping off all of my clothes and sleeping outside to prove she was nothing but a shackle. Which is pretty foolish, considering everything at my feet was laid there because of her. And she was the only parent left at this point. Her boyfriend came out and got me, handed me a blanket, and told me to come inside. When my trichotillomania left me looking like Gollum from Lord of the Rings, she took me to the hair salon, spending thousands to ensure my image was nothing less than a reflection of beautiful sanity. Disguising any imperfection, the same woman who kept me on laxatives since the age of 8 to make sure the only weight on me was there by necessity.

Chapter Eleven

Address the dress tussling on the floor next to a bottle with legs bent and sore, and clean up the mess. It is the greatest chore, for broken glass left unattended will surely cut the unsuspected.

21 September 2017

The curriculum did not require full attendance. Homework was a suggestion at best; in class, it was suggested that getting ice cream in the mall would teach me more than re-evaluating The Great Gatsby for the third time in a different school. On my way out, my phone buzzed with a Facebook message. Nobody uses Facebook anymore. "Did you hear about Stephanie?"

Her Facebook page was message after message of rest in peace. She will be missed. She was taken too soon, a description of a fatal car accident. I've never lost someone before. She wouldn't be there for any of the next five minutes, ten minutes, or five years.

Alone in this bathroom with 1000 different

versions of myself, but none of them is me, and they're all screaming really loudly, a build of mental paroxysm. The only one quiet is the one that she helped cultivate, loss is silent. She's standing amongst the crowd with sand on her feet. I'm swelling.

Synonyms for the word "temporary" include perishable, ephemeral, transitory, and fugitive. Nullable objects must have value even in a state of fleeting consciousness. Synonyms exist, but no two words are alike, each differing in association, connotations, and ever so slightly different meanings and tones. We are all just a bunch of metaphysical words. Her singular word, more. For the world is less without her in it.

Spain has been home for a year now. Hell, we haven't even moved houses; the school was progressive, and I even joined the debate team. The theory of knowledge class in IB (International Baccalaureate) made me realise the value of intelligence and how understanding and addressing something may be a greater alternative than running away from it—the final assignment to ask and answer a question. Don't get me wrong, running away is still my preferred choice of coping; however, this was an opportunity to speak for the unspoken in a country praised for drinking to forget.

Respite

Have you ever had a fascinating conversation with a stranger where they tell you about their life or a moment of impact that will stick with them in their happiest moments and their darkest days— the bumps and bruises? It's because they sat with it like an old friend, pulling up chairs and pouring a glass of wine. Laugh at its absurdity and cry over the loss of innocence, accepting that it is the art of change. Confronting trauma is a lot like confronting an old friend. It will always sink like a lead-filled ship if you aren't grateful for your growth. My brother cries a lot; physically, he overindulges in the stereotypical masculine man covered in tattoos of flames and skulls, compared to a UFC fighter more than most UFC fighters, but every time he drinks, he's right back there with his old friend, and his old friend is kicking the shit out of him; he's on the floor and can't get up because that's what happens when we only talk to our friend when we're drunk.

To hold the attention of a room with words once deemed too weak to wear. I spoke of the times my body was not my own. Tumultuous thoughts trapped inside, containing a power only a few wield, finally crisp bespoke sanity.

You can go on a rant about the expressions of energy whilst sipping your matcha latte as your fedora shades your eyes from the light, though it is not our energy that puts the tension in our attention. It is the captivating audience to whom we speak.

A comedian can do the same skit in one city and be met with only silence and a riot of laughter in another. Would that not stand to reason? Then we do the same with ourselves. As our mindset changes and progresses, our internal audience stands in ovation for one second and, years later, reflects on how we behaved and is met with only disgust and a silent room. So, in turn, should we not encourage the person we have become up to this point to be the one who wields the power to listen, adapt, and act, and let us be surrounded by those who do the same? It is through this we can conquer our environment.

The audience that stood before me knew the weight of words. The truest test of a good person is knowing you can be bad and consciously make the right decision. Simply put, good isn't good when given the choice to be anything but. From 13-18, you are tested and moulded consistently. Experiencing events for the first time, losing your virginity to life.

"At what point does instinct meet reason?"

I can no longer say the word "*rape.*" The word leaves a knot in my throat and forms pressure behind my eye; it almost lacks logic. If you look up the definition, the second meaning via the dictionary is the soiling of a place, doesn't that leave a foul taste in your mouth.

The microphone fumbled in my hands as hundreds of eyes and ears turned to me. "One in four—that's 25 percent." Gesturing to a quarter of the room, I asked, "Will you please stand up?" Making sure that looked right, "That's the number of recorded assaults within the population; thank you, please sit down. It comes down to choice; our instincts guide our wants, and our reason determines what's best. So why is it that in the act of committing a sexual assault, the animalistic instinct to procreate overshadows our reasoning of what is right and wrong? It is not a question of what has happened for thousands of years of inflicting pain and taking; it is a question of self-righteousness, pleasure, and power. Pleasure and power are biological and instinctual; righteousness is solidified through reason."

If my actions were so bold, my words would come out something like this. "Being assaulted diluted what sex meant to me; it was a reaction rather than a response. You won't be able to explain why certain things make you feel better about it, like ashes sprouting daisies. Running away from it and towards something else allowed me to deal with it in parts rather than all at once, which is what most people will try to force you to do with therapy and other institutionalised methods. Fuck that and fuck them; in fear of having to confront it, most women and men would rather keep it to themselves and tuck it away forever. Learn to say the wound is fresh, and all that's needed is antiseptic, time, and maybe a plan B."

Fixate on the strength that comes from knowing above all else you are meant for you; there's no space to caudle or care for another when you're not ready, for my support system has always been reliant on my ability to be greater than any one thing, idea, or event. Be excited to meet the person who allowed something traumatic to evolve them rather than use it as a reason to self-destruct, or maybe I am just blindly delusional by my own idea that "I'm all the better because a collapsing bridge of sanity toxically strengthens me."

I'm not going to talk about forgiveness because it's a deceptively bad argument. We don't have to forgive anybody. Forgive the man who thought it was a good idea to laugh at my vulnerability and abuse it. Outrageous, if given a chance, I'd break his nose with a giggle and patch him up because his mother doesn't need to see him bruised, even though mine did. It just comes down to accepting what your life is. It's the same as being insecure about your body. You can only make the most of it, and the more you spend time dwelling, the bigger your friend gets and the smaller you become. Instead of spending time trying to forgive your trespassers, say, "Thank you for the lesson," and move on. Even healed wounds turn into scars when they're deep enough.

People like to use logic to justify behaviours, but the most logical thing of all is that logic only operates as a conduit for desire, directing its path towards justification, and in hindsight, that's kind of unnecessary because it doesn't change the outcome. Sometimes you're just a statistic.

Just maybe after today, one less person won't have to go through it.

Chapter Twelve

Punctured Armour

So, we've reached that part—the part that dreads being written and read in woeful disdain. The thing that every song, movie, late-night conversation, poet, and artist fails to express truly is that if it were articulated in a way that made sense, we wouldn't spend so much time trying to figure out what it was. The first attribute of love that we are taught is security. When we take that first tumble and are held close, comforted in times of exposed fragility, the reflection of how someone else's actions make us feel, but love is a fickle thing; it holds us in a place of consistency, and yet we never really know when it begins.

A man whose name I only heard in conversations about recklessness said, "I like my world, and you can be a part of it, but you'll never be the main character."

My stomach aches are consoled in the comfort of my bed, far more endearing company than any person, bad jokes, or nihilistic conversations that could be held at a party until my friend told me about one at the residence of the aforementioned man.

He strummed Better together by Jack Johnson on the guitar, pausing at the appearance of new arrivals, he could have continued encapsulated in the rhythmic dance of his fingers dancing along the neck, but what kind of host lingers on their hellos. The two kisses you give when you greet someone in Europe have never felt sweeter. The night ended the moment he came into view. This house rager only consisted of about eight people. My closest friends and a stranger who showed me spots on a map of where he likes to go spearfishing and me reliving my favourite dive footage, the first time talking about my fish in over a year. The low muffle of conversations undisturbed by his playlist shuffling through songs that bleed nostalgia. There it was, the beauty of the blossoming tree. A movement so fast it was motionless and like a tree it evolved into a being that owed us nothing, but gave us everything.

I've never cared whether or not someone held an interest in me, but here I was, still pestered by thoughts of him after a month of silence. I'm debating going out and stealing a car just to not be bored of this mundane life.

Tinder the Tenderiser

Artificial selection collides with affairs of the heart. Before, we would have butterflies in the presence of our person, and their reactions were a reflection of their attentiveness now as we sit and scroll, craving just a slimmer of that flutter. The magic has been sent back into the world, absorbed by the trees, waiting for our technological tendency to pass so that we may experience the raw beauty of organic love. But who knows what will bloom when it is not the seed; just the sun and water?

There he was. Zamir. His profile was a picture of him on his bike, the helmet barely covering his smile. You got to experience it only if you saw it in person, which was a worthy sight. It took me six hours to go back online every 20 minutes to see his helmet again.

Really, That's It?

You see, there's this rule someone taught me to follow about being on time, and right at 9:00 p.m, we met next to my shiny Alfa Romeo. He offered to pick me up, but who could resist showing off something so pretty? Every movement was a distraction, possibly done with as much intent as he displayed. The flex of his arm or the twitch of his foot—was it discomfort, anticipation, desire, or solely an unconscious stretch? Maybe that's too much credit, as my slight lean inward or accidental foot touches, flicks of my hair, or slight brush of my leg are meant to be sent as an indication of my willingness to partake in the game of his choosing, thinking he holds my king in check. However, it is my queen lying in wait.

"Dates are usually uncomfortable for me; it's just a lot of talking, which I don't think I'm very good at." That's not entirely true; it's just not as comfortable as cutting to the point of who is taking off their clothes first. "Have you ever had a boyfriend?" good question, "No, have you?" lifting his glass, "No, I've never had a boyfriend." The man thinks he's funny. "Never had a girlfriend either." Society's enigmas, while others were getting into relationships, we were busy getting into trouble.

The night continued until he walked me to my car, then he kissed me. He just kissed me. No one had ever just kissed me to feel my lips against theirs, and damn, his were soft. His hand wrapped around my face—a drug worth craving. It wasn't Adderall, weed, Xanax, or even the thrill of travelling that could compare to the rush of this feeling of wanting more and not getting it. Maybe ecstasy came close, which makes that word make a lot more sense, but this was organically simulated endorphins. What an odd date.

I'll Bite

There were no sharks, diving expeditions, or flights to catch; the moments where normal meant boring. A ride on my longboard down the path that hugged the sea created a calming kind of relief. It was my alone time, except today, my solitude held company— him. Just two people skating under the moon, revealing scars and wounds unhealed. If the world was mute, the significance of a look wouldn't change. Again, just a kiss.

For She's a Jolly Good Fellow
28 April 2018

He was the king of the plastic toy castle along that same stretch of dirt called the Paseo. Amidst telling him a story about how my tooth was fake and cracked big enough to stick a whole cigarette in it, he asked me why my travels started so young and never seemed to stop. He got the whole story that night, cocking his head and raising his eyebrows. We spoke about religion, too. "Scientifically speaking, matter cannot be created nor destroyed; therefore, this is heaven, hell, and purgatory cycling through stardust. We could be reborn as butterflies, an animal that cannot speak, for words can be foul." He would be the biggest and most beautiful butterfly of all. Wings big enough to rest upon. Feeding into my foolishness, he proclaimed, "We can flutter around in people's stomachs, making the world a beautiful ray of fucking sunshine."

With him, I'm Belle. She has a Southern accent, rides horses topless in a field in spring, and smiles at a text message. The audacity to have such power. She is soft and vulnerable, emitting holy light, divine and warm, like a hot bath of sunshine, and that's how he made me feel. He took me home, and before the door opened, my top was already off. A good start to a birthday if you're into that kind of thing.

On the first day of May, when birds sing and spring merges with summer, at one o'clock in the morning, a notification read, "I'm in the hospital; I broke both my legs today." That motherfucker. This is it: you finally start to like a guy for more than a night, and he ends up in a hospital. Maybe I'm better off alone, as my luck doesn't seem to extend beyond good weather and spontaneous trips.

Nine days since his accident, three days since he's been off morphine, and two days till he's released. He won't let me see him, and it's starting to piss me off. Not only has every other guy failed to compare to him, but now he is beginning to take up too much space in my head, robbing me of days of peace. Where I'm from, burglars get shot.

He was allowed two days of being home, rolling around in his wheelchair, before I showed up with toy helicopters in hand. His mattress was spread out in his living room to make it more accessible. He bought us steaks, which he angrily tried to cook on a countertop that was a little too high. Until chef Tea chose to intervene. I'm being domesticated. Every task required energy he didn't have, and worse, he hated asking for help. So I gave him a task that did not require any.

After a month, he dropped his chair and could pick me up again. This continued for months, falling deeper and deeper into the rabbit hole. In times of pain, he would listen; when my insecurities blossomed into anger, he would make me laugh. This was uncharted territory that could not be conquered but only observed.

This is love, fuck. "I've fallen in love with you, and as the first man that has ever had the privilege of me saying those words to him, you ought to know just how extraordinary this moment is. My realisation and your gratification for such a monumental prize." His breath was held while mine was taken away. "Please don't say it back; this isn't about you even if you do. For the longest time, I didn't know if I could fall in love, yet here we are. You have shown me myself in rose-coloured glasses."

A face to a name, a look to a feeling, a gesture to an embrace. The steps for my first fall. The name of a man who was in pieces on a pedestal made of sand brought about my soft-spoken Belle.

We only have so much energy to give, though. Don't we act like it is a bottomless pit of giving, a well that never dries? Here was this man, draped in legacy. In some twisted way, he matched and surpassed my convoluted, tenebrous family with his own. Is that what love shall be for me. Damn the damned, with more damage caused within that lies my deserving love. Vengeance of the heart truly.

"Mom, have you seen my black Jimmy Choos?"

"I can't hear you; I'm downstairs." They were always under the bed. Slipping them on as Cinderella would if her taste extended to something comfortable and fashionable. It was graduation day—the first one I've ever had. My mother sat in a crowd amongst friends who knew not everything but the product of years of trying to find the little space where a piece fits. Everything was coming to an end. Your brain constructs the existence of everything around you, and there was a moment after my certificate was handed where my eyes shut just long enough to tell my brain that my dad was sitting there in that crowd too.

2 July 2018

We got picked up again. Just because my dads case ended didn't mean my mothers did. Something had happened in Italy.

Indonesia, my next stop, sailing through the Komodo Islands, dropping B.R.U.V.S. and counting indicator species, with a return date of only two days before my university classes begin in the Caribbean. Five days left in Spain—five days left with him.

On the last day before my departure, he showed me the purest form of him, alone in a world of our own, dancing to our own tune away from the drowning noise of others. The sex pushed boundaries, leaving marks on my cheeks (all of them) and biting me with no tender intent. He liked the security of condoms and finishing with me; he didn't fuck with an objective. He fucked to feel. Draping his dick in honey to mask the chemical latex taste was bittersweet. Plopped the spoon right back in the jar without a second thought. When our time was over and done, my mouth was full of him. He walked over to the jar of honey with the spoon sticking out and said, "We cannot leave this here." The thought of someone using honey that had remnants of him contaminating the jar, callously mixing honey into tea—honey that shared the same taste that lingers in my mouth still.

"Stop that." He caught me with hands wrapped up in my hair, grabbed them, and pulled them into his curly nest. "There, play with me instead." plopping his head down in my lap and turning my world upside down. That was when he asked about my return in the winter and if maybe he could be an unwrapped present on my return home for Christmas. He spoke to the ceiling and to a girl who didn't exist because my family does not celebrate Christmas, and I've never returned to a country I've left with packed bags. Love is a well-kept secret, treasured most brightly in a dark room. That's why God put the Ten Commandments in stone, right? For if something is not declared, it is an assumption; immoral beings assume the worst so that we can hope for the best. It is a moral conflict: To grasp the extent of your own force, limits must be written in steel. Prosecuting a commandment of your deliberate intention and intending to break no hearts, especially my own, by pretending to be capable of something unachievable. So, at this moment, he will lay encompassed in the fleeting feeling only I give him.

It was love, for what love was scripted to be, and once again, saying goodbye, and I was the only one who heard it. Men are not a necessity but one hell of an accessory; the fairytale is the standard held now, and this is why young love is fated to die because life goes on; there are flowers to be picked, after all.

Today Ended An Hour Ago

Cloud

Not trying to catch you
This isn't a game of ball
So why do you look at me
With such a fear to fall
Is it that I might be a cloud
Full and far too high
Simply meant to look upon
When your eyes meet the sky

For if I am a cloud, does that make you rain
You being a product of what I contain
What is it you think I seek
Maybe you are a bird simply passing by
With feathers of lead that won't let you fly

Does my colour catch the light
Do I dance to your winds of might
It is not that I am asking what I am to you
For I am not easy to mold
And much like a cloud unable to hold

Chapter Thirteen

Bandaids

My life had become a series of snippets, clips taken from an old movie directed by my passport and my mother's conspiratorial affairs. The airport here is full of Americans and tourists; locals are called locals because they don't leave.

You can genuinely see the experienced versus the inexperienced. Travelling is necessary for many reasons, but here are the top 10.

Ten reasons to travel:

1. "Things" are unnecessary. The value placed on commercial goods becomes apparent when lugging around a 20-pound duffle bag with you every day.
2. You begin to assume that people are ignorant and explain everything in greater detail, forcing you to be smarter and more confident with your knowledge without even knowing it.

3. Culture can only be as authentic as its origin. Would you describe a fruit as fresh after spending days on a plane being relocated? Dilute your ignorance.
4. Experience is the mother of knowledge. Home can be found in the pages of a book, the hug of a friend, or a cup of tea, because it's everything you carry with you.
5. Food, those fancy cheeses you buy in the States, claiming to be imported from so and so. Well, once you remove the imported part, replace it with authentically locally-sourced produce. There is no going back.
6. People, you don't know who your people are until you have met who your people aren't.
7. Self-discovery: That feeling that you're destined for something great only comes from leaving your comfort zone and finding out what you're great at.
8. Value of a dollar: the value of a dollar changes everywhere you go, so choose where you spend your days wisely for it is not the only currency you exchange.

9. Religion plays on the fear of the unknown. If you fuck my wife, you will spend all of eternity suffering, having your nails pried off one by one whilst being bathed in a vat of hellfire.
10. Thrift stores are a long-term traveller's best friend. There's always at least one or two places that sell second-hand clothing for a dollar or, max, five. Not only do you get authentic local wear, but you can find really cool shit there too. My favourite was this long needle-strap handmade dress covered in patches of different patterns with a little knot in the back to tighten around the boobies.

There was business to attend to in Vancouver, my documents needed to be renewed. I stopped in San Francisco to do some intermittent healing. Apple had always offered her place as a space to be if things ever got rough again. We haven't kept in touch just to let each other know that we love each other and think about each other but never actually talk about what happened. Some friends don't require constant intervention or play-by-plays of your life to know they will always be there.

It was a week before Fathers Day (18th June). A day that had gone uncelebrated and unappreciated for many years now. His number has always been the same; the only difference was that this was the first time my number would pop up on his phone as an incoming call. "I'm sorry, Tea; wish you had told me sooner. I'm going on a trip with the guys. You remember them...." He started listing off names of his buddies that held no significance right now because he was busy after six years apart and finally being in the same state, hell, the same time zone, and the same continent. Rejection is a feeling I have become accustomed to on the rare occasion of conversing with him, maybe the thought that the people who love us will drop everything to be there is just a narcissistic expectation. He spoke in words of admiration to everyone else; *Look at what my daughter has done. She dives with sharks. She's travelled the world.* Yet to me, he is scorned with the anger of my absence for not staying and testifying on his behalf, but I'd be dead, and there would be no one to testify.

Everything was the same as when the wheels touched down on my old stomping ground. Apple picked me up from the airport, looking as foggy as it was outside, with four new pieces of metal sticking out of her face. "Hey, babe, you starting to look like a pincushion." Unimpressed by her witty observation, I said, "Feel like one too."

Not everybody has someone to validate that it wasn't just you as a woman getting passed around, not just in a physical sense, with eyes, skeevy thoughts, holding only the value of entertainment. Look with different eyes and learn a little more about your relationship with sex. A bad first experience diluted what sex was, and that was a comforting crutch. Letting go of a tiny bit of anger today was noticeable. There are enough spiteful apparitions in this country.

It was a nice time; sometimes, that's all something has to be, but it's a shame when it could have been more. It could've been a time when we talked about it, cried, hugged each other, acknowledged and healed, but instead, we wound up in another person's basement drinking Smirnoff. It was a community that was small but not close. At least my last memories here won't be bad ones; then it dawned on me.

Holy shit, I'm back in this bed, in that room. Not even angry because I'm not her anymore. The light from my phone lit a face that couldn't stop smiling. Chess has become my companion, and with some artificial intelligence crafted through intricate coding, my opponent and the genius sitting at a little laptop in my brain came up with a brilliant idea. Click on Marc in your contacts and send him a link to play chess. You crafty son of a bitch.

We didn't have to speak at all; just played on that common ground. He would learn if he didn't know, and this is how we move forward—one step at a time. The biggest person isn't always the oldest in the room.

Chapter Fourteen

Law-Abiding Citizens

4 October 2019

The beautification team in the Caribbean enjoys placing trees in the middle of the road to remind tourists they are on an island surrounded by pillars of towering ambience as they speed by in the Jeep Wrangler rented to experience the Shaka lifestyle. My classes were nothing but a requirement for attention and an easy finish to my dive master certification. The sea is a home that never fails expectations; the real lessons learned were taught to me by the people of the Caribbean on an island no bigger than a small town, 32 kilometres from point A to point B.

Hurricane Maria drowned what Irma didn't decimate. Over the hill towards Redhook was a two-storey church sliced in half like a cadaver, with splintered wooden walls and pieces of window barely holding on, like a Tuesday afternoon stripper. It wasn't a pretty sight. The weather was never something to pay much attention to; everything seemed to work out in my favour.

There was news that NASA spent over 100 million dollars developing a pen to write in space, and when the Russians arrived in space, confronted with the same problem of a standard pen not working, they used a pencil. Now this likely being a hoax, however, poses a confounding method of ideology. As one could say, the Russians succeeded because they chose the simpler path by using pre-existing materials. On the other hand, you may say NASA prevailed as it saw the value of the pen over the value of the pencil. A pen being permanent allows all mistakes to be visible. No thought is bad, as thoughts equal progression, valuing knowledge as a process, not just a product, like a car and a mechanic.

I got a job at a surf shop, attended my classes, and lived an exceptionally extraordinary version of the ordinary. When my car broke down, a new one didn't just reappear; she had to be taken into the shop.

The brakes on my Chevy S10 had been soft-pedalling for about a week. The mechanic is on the other side of the island, and there's a really steep hill to venture over, and without brakes, it's risky. My old cum shot passed the broken-down gas station with the pervy clerk, up the whining road past the thrift store, and down that shitty, not-so-little hill across from half a church. Braking as hard as possible, though, really didn't make much of a difference. A smart person would have gotten a tow truck—correction: a responsible person would've, and a reckless individual like myself manages to stay only a few inches from every car in front.

A litter of little puppies ambushed me at the entrance. The runt, bathed in black and white with only three little legs—three and a half—tucked herself under a big truck. A wire in the fence must have taken it clean off, as it still looked a little infected; it must've been recent. There are so many strays on the island that the locals don't really participate when they're seen walking around. They had a big bowl of food, but the responsibility extending beyond that was too much, and there were so many, but this little trilateral was mine. My car got fixed, and so did she. We stopped by the weed store on the way home. In my apartment, I rolled my joint, brought Mako into the bathtub, blasted some Whitney Houston, and scrubbed all the nasty shit that followed her home on her back.

Phytoplankton

"Please tell me you can entertain me because I'm drowning in restlessness."

Zahmir and I talked on occasion, but it was nothing exciting. When you have something truly special, it doesn't translate to a mobile edition. In person, it's authentic, whereas over the phone, it feels forced. On the occasions when I find myself back at the mechanic, I send him photos of the engines and tell him what I'm working on, but a conversation over the phone is just a reminder you're not together.

Mako is being extra fussy; she won't lay down and watch our favourite movie Mulan, regardless of the epic playlist and finest Disney love interest. The sun was about to say goodnight, and that was her favourite time to go outside, but her bark was more of an alarm than anything else; the only thing that could get her this excited was when iguanas trespassed onto the porch. But we just finished iguana hunting season, so there really weren't that many around. It might sound cruel, but there are a lot of these fuckers here, and they're vicious. I followed her to the front, and there he was, standing in my doorway. There's a that saying if you love something, set it free, and if it was meant to be, it would return to thee. It never felt real, like poetry, but that's because nothing has ever come back.

"Surprise, baby."

"What are you doing here? I have a guy over." His face dropped, like his worst fear of what could've happened had come true.

"I'm joking." Pressing his face into mine, wrapping my legs around him as had been done so many times before. Even after soaking in the humidity, he still smelled of rust.

His bags took up space in the room that was now ours for the next 48 hours.

We drove down that road to my favourite secret spot that you can only get to by hiking down a path, not for the tender-footed to a cove guarded by the cliffs and trees. Moonlight filled the sea as if it was the size of a bathroom sink, but not enough to hide the phytoplankton bloom. Phytoplankton comes from the Greek word "phyton plankton", meaning plant drifter (φυτόν πλαγκτός). For a moment, as the water pooled in our hands, we held something that could otherwise not be held. We were disturbing the delicate ecosystem's primary food source to shower each other with the light it emitted.

Do microscopic organisms fall in love too, or is that only reserved for hearts big enough to break? We went home to play house and give ourselves a glimpse of a life neither of us was made for. If my love story was better, let it not bend to the sands of time.

Love changes us, and we experience moments that otherwise wouldn't have existed. Their interests become important to us because they make up who they are, and we love the characteristics that make them. Good, bad, indifferent—these are fleeting interpretations that change our opinion. People make time comprehensive. In solitude, their fluidity is structured under our control. Add another person to the equation, and there is an uncontrollable variable: right time, right person, wrong place.

My hyper-dramatic side kind of wishes there was some big fight where he would storm off, and I would get to throw my head back in disbelief at his outrageous accusations of me cheating with my butler, or maybe one of my professors, and I could say something to beg for his forgiveness like, "*I will try and tell you what I know you need me to say. What you feel my actions fail to convey. I will tell you how your smile never evades my eyes, for it's brighter and rarer than the sun. How when I envision a partner, it's reflected in the way your hand folds into mine. The person I was before you came into my life lies deep within me, and I hope never to make her acquaintance again. It is not that I lean on your existence like a man with a cane. It is that you are a balloon that lifts me away, and falling for you was the first time I fell forwards."*

Sadly, no. The worst thing to happen was when we would order food and I would ask him how long it would take, and he would look at the screen when it would say 15-25 minutes, and he would say the minimum number. You don't do that; that builds a false expectation. You say the maximum amount of time it would take so that when it comes sooner, there is joy instead of anger at the thought that your food is late.

"Fuck off, my love, and have a safe flight."

Eventually, after you do something repeatedly, its significance is significantly diluted. If chess can represent life, then intimacy and saying goodbye were the English opening of my beloved game, and it was time to resign. He would fall in love again with someone more convenient who saw his smile for exactly what it was—home, words drawn from a blank canvas.

He left that day with no inclination to return; our

paths may cross again, but like the plankton in the sea you just have to move with the current and the only remaining now is our footprints in the sand. Call it a gut feeling; his smile, which felt like a hug, flew away with him.

In certain ways, the ways in which we are uncertain of loving ourselves, we hire someone else to do it.

The Cycle

For the longing nights, I lay awake

I smell the scents that remind me of you

The touch of your hand in mine and your inconsistent breathes

For your face changes and you become many

As I continue to fall in and out of love,

You are not you but a feeling,

Something I can not grab or hold on to

Materialised by fantasies

You are something I find

For you are loved and lost and loved again

Chapter Fifteen

Somedays, Sometimes, Somewhere, Someone, Something

January 2020

People talk about the calm before the storm, the sun that comes to illuminate and cast shadows, the calm winds, and the undisturbed leaves. All were lying in wait for the catastrophe brewing, but hell, people talk about anything these days just to hear themselves speak.

How far will you go to impersonate the person you desperately want to be?

You can tell how long someone has lived in a house by the number of spoons, cups, and silverware they have—nicknacks and a collection of symbols for memories not forgotten. Meiko's godmother lives on Water Island, which is just a three-dollar and five-minute ferry ride away. Sometimes she loves her more than me; when we fight, I threaten to send her over there, and to be honest, she understands me and patiently waits for the day when she adopts her because her house has full roaming privileges. She's spending the weekend with her because my mom called to meet her in Jamaica. Our old family rules still apply, even though I'm 20 now. Do as you are told; once done, you may ask why.

The flight was short enough but borderline hazardous. No plane like a seaplane to make you never fly again. The sea in the Caribbean from the sky was brighter and bluer than any painting could do it justice. Our family here were politicians, legacy babies, doctors, lawyers, and architects. Jamaica runs on a class system, and we were at the top of it. The driver picked me up from the airport to bring me to my aunties' home at the top of Sunflower Road. Just bank left at the Devon House ice cream shop and go all the way up.

"Baby, look how dark you got; you're a mess. Do you even shower anymore? Laying up in the sun like it won't destroy that beautiful skin I gave you," she said, gripping my chin and looking into my eyes as if she had to check that my body was actually mine and not replaced with a shifty pod person. "I just got off the plane, mama, and what about you? You look like you haven't slept in a month." Her eyes were puffy and dropping. She was bloated and swollen from her head to her toes. "I'm just sick; haven't been feeling well. That's not true; my mother never got sick. Not once growing up did she catch the flu; her immune system could fight off a plague.

"Go shower; then Maria will cook you some ackee and saltfish." Maria was the chef, and I wasn't joking about the strict class system here. The only time you spoke to them was when you wanted something. I've never been very good at obeying that tradition, though, getting stern looks from my grandmother every time we were caught laughing in the kitchen, but she never raised her voice as that would be unladylike.

My mother's phone wouldn't stop interrupting my peaceful shower. Wrapping my hair up to see the menace causing such disturbances, I saw 15 missed calls from her boyfriend. *Sorry, husband.* I figured I'd send him a message saying she was with my grandmother downstairs, but it never got to that, for the disturbance in my day was far greater than the ringing of a phone. The last message read, "I booked my ultrasound for this week. Wish you were here to see the first images of him." She's fucking pregnant at the age of 54; can she not do anything according to the normal rules of life?

Retire, settle down, and get another cat if you must. I was still wrapped up in my towel, preparing to confront a mama bear.

"You're pregnant." The whole house turned their eyes to my mama. Especially my grandmother, until she turned to me and said, "Hush now, don't you raise your voice to your mother nand go put on some clothes," grabbing my arm and turning me over. That was all the confirmation I needed, and I was no longer confused about the unexpected trip to Jamaica for the weekend.

Thoughts of her in jail cell pregnant, the restraints caught on the ultrasound table. Have you ever cried wrapped up in a towel? It's all very dramatic. The metal jingling rang in my ear. Not that she would be in jail for longer than a week; she always came home. So there will be nights when it doesn't matter who gets hurt because, in the end, they will be stronger for it, colder to the world, and either crave the chaos they were brought up in or do everything within their power to build that white picket fence. The name they will be born with will not be their only one.

She would sit stroking his hair, singing *Lemon tree, very pretty, and the lemon flower is sweet. Bbut the fruit of the poor lemon is impossible to eat,* a folk song by Peter

Paul and Mary we all grew up with, dreaming of who he would be: a doctor, a lawyer, a businessman, an athlete. It's about what money can't buy, Mom. The jewels on her neck were not her accessories but us, the people she brought into this world. Her little sapling, what fruit will you bear?

Chapter Sixteen

To Sin or Not to Sin Which Decision Shall Win

It is ironic that Saint Thomas is located in the Virgin Islands because there is no purity to be found here. The sea is cleaner than the people, a sinner in all of us escaping through destructive addictions, the devil on our shoulders—provoking dysfunction when ignored by the other voices in our heads. Born of experience, stress-tolerant individuals often talk to their sinner because you might have an IQ of 105, but they might have an IQ of 140, and if you exile them, you ignore the driving potential they carry. Sinners run away even when no one is chasing them, Proverb 28, but how do you know you won't end up somewhere breathtaking without seeing it for yourself, Teaha 20.

The invitation to feed that part of myself always finds its way into my mailbox. I'm not shiny; just bruised, scratched, and maybe not that bright. There is no tool that exists that can polish out these dents. Not damaged, just complicated, but who would ever want to be simple? Every shaping moment, every moment worth having, should force a shift in your perspective and be something that is complex, something that is ever-changing.

Acknowledging which variables are constant, leaving the rest as unknown. Time, a constant in and of itself, is the division of distance over speed. How far will you go, and how fast will you do it?

The gods are envious of us for our mortality, and we envy them for their power to take it away.

The litter of pups that used to swarm me left as they all grew up, but one stuck around; they call him Pigeon. He hangs out in the back room with the boss, in the principal's office, only to be called in when you've done something wrong. The garage, where rowdy nature lingers and does not reflect any garage as everything but the office is outside, cars covered only by metal canopies: big cars, big tools, all big toys for big boys. My femininity was clouded, foggy, and drowning in the masculine image created around them. Ten feet tall, in a heavy-duty 450 Ford, your size becomes nothing; of course, they wouldn't let me drive her. How often do we forget that we're driving when behind the wheel? In a car, your impact is extended to something much greater than what we are accustomed to. Power, horsepower, baby, and it puts people on edge. A gun sticking out of a pocket can look a lot like a wrench until uncovered, and here it is as vital as every other tool that lies in this shop.

We can call him John, a big guy with a heavy breath. When he sat in a chair, the chair sat with him. I don't know if that was his real name, as he had a woman come around every so often who called him Romeo, but she was no Juliet. Not a great guy to owe money to, but you see, with John, he was also an opportunist in and outside the office.

You'd think with me coming around as often as I did learning about coils and exhausts, different engine types, what the hell a piston operated on, what kind of shaft did that thing that shafts do, he would start to look at me with kinder eyes. Instead, he took it as an opportunity to try and increase my monthly car bill. There are measures put in place to keep the greedy at bay, and we call them laws. In the Caribbean, they are more of a suggestion; people spoke more openly about what was going on and kept things coherent in a lot of ways. Extortion isn't a pretty word, just an ugly action. My momma handled it as she always had. Just a phone call, and John never bothered me again. Occasionally I would get the question, *"How is she doing?"* It didn't matter who you were or are; it means nothing to someone who cares for nought.

The Princess, the Shepherd, and the Mule

Once upon a time, there was a princess who had not one but many castles to play in. Each was filled with art, wardrobes matching in size, gardens that bloomed regardless of the season, and servants to cater to even the most obscene requests. One day, the princess ventured off on a tour of neighbouring kingdoms in search of a rare diamond to add to her collection. Now this diamond is said to bestow a feeling on the beholder, none of which has ever been felt, and to look upon it is to see beyond the stars and into the smallest vein of a leaf. The carriage this day was set to be her finest, big enough to house six full men, yet she sat alone, letting her only company be the autumn winds.

About a day's ride in, the princess happened upon an injured man on the road, a shepherd. She opened the door, scolding him for intervening in her journey as he pleaded for aid. Demanding assistance, he is the shepherd who tends to all the sheep whose wool keeps her warm in the coldest of winters, and if he does not make it home in time, the sheep shall go unsheared and his family unfed.

Bargaining with something more than time wasted, she spoke above the crippled man, for he had nothing but words and a mule that carried his value. A great secret, and upon his safe return home, he would share it.

As the shepherd returned to his lands, he left her with these words: "A shepherd's responsibility is to tend, lead, and guard. To be a shepherd is to be human on this day; you are henceforth a shepherd." Despite her arrogance, he gifted her his mule and a smile. She departed, more disgusted than grateful for a half-blind companion barely strong enough to carry her baggage.

As night fell, the carriage made it to the first kingdom where nothing but bad news was found, and that was certainly no diamond or the sought-after feeling. Her tale of woe and empty endeavours continued until the moon's face showed the same as it did the night she first met her mule. Angry and defeated, she kicked and yelled a royal tantrum. In her heightened break, she shoved her mule off the cliff. The sky was bright, and as he fell, she stared into his eye, the one that held no sight, but she saw his vision. Hope. Her humanity fell with him as the last lingering link to the only remotely good deed she had ever done. A fate worse than death is to lose what makes you human. This does not come with negative insight, for the feeling she embodied was unlike any other. She let go of humanity and became more. Rotten by her capabilities, she felt everything and nothing. When the noise that fluttered in her head quieted, she turned to find the mule in place of her carriage, his sight restored, and resting in her hand an eye that burned white and sparkled like a diamond.

She spoke unto the lands, "Hello little flowers waiting to bloom until the spring rains smell of honeysuckle. You are washed and prepared for the annual awakening, but the sun never shows its blinding smile. You wait until fate decides when your petals may touch something other than themselves, nuzzling petal atop petal. Your roots are laid deep, grounded to the earth that germinated its seedy self. Amongst the tumultuous rain, you sprout thorns, defending until the day you realise the sun was always there; you were just in the shade." She took off her crown and walked into a new world as a half-sighted mule and as a shepherd that tended to wilted flowers.

4 June 2020

Coffee, cigarettes, and a good view of my consistency through the years. I had the oddest dream last night, as if someone had painted a broken heart and shoved it in my chest. My coffee burned, and the clouds blocked the sea from my window. I guess the only repetition today will be found in the slighted conversation with the trees. They listen to beggars and the wealthy, so their knowledge knows no bounds. We had a fallout once when they refused to hear me. Maybe I spoke too softly. Have you ever been ignored by a tree? The shade no longer dances side to side and the leaves remain attached to their dominating space. Perched on an extended branch that hung next to the orange tree in the garden reading from a collection of manga on my tablet. Perhaps it was my outward longing to live amongst a world engulfed by surrealism that was met with silence. How ignorant of me to not realize trees might prefer realism. Yes, I shall play some Fleetwood Mac for her tomorrow to make up for my incompetence. I leave some leftover peanuts where the roots begin to dive and Mako's water bowl below where my feet would dangle from the branch so she may have company in my absence.

Today feels stained by ink that is only loyal to the soiled.

There's this little bar next to Chicken 'n Bowling that serves three-dollar Jager bombs; those have always been a favourite. Before I could even walk in, my friends began shoving shots in my face. "To the world's shittiest diver." What did he even know about diving? He was a physics major. "To the world's shittiest friends, love you all." Thursday nights are trivia night, and it can get ridiculously violent.

1. How many hearts does an octopus have?
   Answer: Three
2. Do sponges have hearts?
   Answer: No
3. Which company owns Bugatti and Lamborghini? Audi, Porsche, and Ducati?
   Answer: Volkswagen

That was the extent of my assistance in a 30-question game.

Winner team, relatively slow. A terrible joke between the physics majors.

The rain smelled of laundry, the kind that hangs out to dry, just like the magnolia tree that still sheds every fall and blossoms every spring, like Mako on days when it would rain and she would get lost in the trees the same scent that stays the same no matter where I end up.

My beautiful blurry cum shot blinked twice, convincing myself that six tequila shots and, well, just call it, X amount of whiskey had no lingering effect on me. Marina climbed in the passenger's seat and put her hand on my leg with a big smile, more than ready to get out of here.

"It's one of your last night as who you are today; we're gonna go fucking hard." Insanity seeping out of drunken eyes and her hand gripping me. I like her. She dances loudly and with her eyes closed. After all, she was taking my position at the surf shop; maybe she was going to be the new Teaha. Let's be honest, though; there's no one like me or her. Nobody's really like anyone; eight billion people, and no two are alike.

The engine started, lurching backwards out of the nook she was tucked away in, completely ignoring the fact that water piled onto my windshield, obstructing all view of the road ahead. Bob Marley on the radio reminds us not to worry about a thing. The car began to hydroplane, dancing over the road, control stripped bare from my hands as the rain raped the reins. A mind flooded by booze is no mind at all, for the gas pedal looks a lot like the brake. Over the curb and into the trunk, my bumper failed to bump, and headlights popped and scattered. Then the hood, engine, and transmission followed in combustion. The unintended obstacle favoured my side in this collision. My forehead met the steering wheel, and then there was darkness, followed by a roaring screech from the tyres. The bent-up metal, folding and crumpling, reformed.

The alarm wont stop blaring, or is that my ears ringing? Vision blurred, one contact left, swelling growing where my forehead kissed the steering wheel, glass falling like rain. "Marina." Marina wailed, clutching her stomach and crying. The deflated airbag crumpled over me, the dust and shards on the dash catching blue and red lights. Doors jam shut and won't open to the sounds of pleading. In an initial release, my feet stumble out around the back. My ankle, fuck my ankles in pieces, cracking every step. People are gathering witnesses to a show without a curtain call. Her side of the distorted door hangs open, seat belt unhooked. "I've got you. I've got you." Her arms wrapped around my neck, taking all of her weight. A man, a light, an occupier of space took her from me. In the wake of havoc, she departed. My feet were folding. "*Are you okay?*' Was my ride an ambulance or a police car? "Yeah, just spun out; called a tow truck. Should be on the way." Satisfied, he left and returned to his life away from the broken scene. My direction now was towards home, my bed, my Mako, but one step in that direction was all that was left at the end of the day. It is similar to blinking but slower and half fulfilled, like pouring a glass of wine as the red spills out of the bottle but never reaches the glass.

I collapsed, waking up surrounded by strangers and with an unforgivable headache.

The saddest word in the English language is "almost". Security almost came in the form of love; peace almost prevailed from an unforgiving place; and I almost walked away from the crash unscathed, but my injury wasn't something a hospital could fix. My memories were taken, some at first and more over time, along with the versions of me created over the years. A part of me did die that day because an insatiable appetite bloomed in my garden. There are a lot of things left to do that will be left undone as that self, but more was seen then unseen. The lingering collsion comes when the wind talks to me, she speaks to all of us and she can get angry when she doesn't feel heard so she roars and topples buildings.

By the age of twenty I had been the american doll cheerleader, the girl who dives with sharks, a quiet observer sipping a coffee in florence, a delinquent in boarding school, a wonderer amongst the mountain sides and through all of this I am left now with another plane ticket, pen and some scratches of paper and a little brother who is soon to enter the world. I am not sure if there is a point to all of this other than to make the most of it, but how inexplicably profound is it that there is so much we may touch and all to add to this story we call life. Risk and reward, the more that has been obtained equates the more that can be lost. That's the beautiful balance.

My Love Letter to you,

We are finite; we have a beginning, middle, and end—a collection of embodied beings.

Look at the life lived thus far with such widened eyes that nothing less than a practically scripted moment could alter the standard you've created. The connection between the main character, Teaha, and the title of this book is that she is an acronym for the time in between. Today Ended An Hour Ago. TEAHA, what is our perception of today, tomorrow, and the day before but an accumulation of thoughts, memories, and passing collisions?

There are gurus, shamans, priests, and a drunken girl in a club on a Saturday night who will all have opinions on how life should be lived. I will fall under the drunk girl category rather than any guru or man you would DMT with in a hut finding yourself in Bali.

I had a car accident in 2020 that left my brain bruised, specifically my prefrontal cortex. My memories began disappearing, but it wasn't until I had my first seizure in 2021 that I nearly erased most of my memories of the past five years. I had always been diligent in writing in journals and trying to recall moments I didn't want to forget, which led me to write this coming-of-age novel.

Thank you to my family for giving me a life worth living, my father who put in the work to mend our relationship, my mother who has extended beyond the ordinary and to my best friend, Anders, for seeing through me, reminding me that family extends beyond blood.

Ingram Content Group UK Ltd.
Milton Keynes UK
UKHW040849100723
424852UK00004B/203